DECEPTIVE

DECEPTIVE

BOOK THREE IN THE ON THE RUN INTERNATIONAL MYSTERIES

SARA ROSETT

DECEPTIVE
Book Three in the *On The Run International Mysteries* series

Second Paperback Edition: November 2016
First Paperback Edition: July 2013

ISBN: 978-0-9982535-7-2

1

March 10, Paris

The woman with long red hair appeared to be leisurely browsing one of the clothing racks in the Paris boutique, but her attention was less focused on the fabric and cut of the dresses than on the art gallery visible through the shop's front window. When a couple, obviously tourists—easily identifiable because of their camera case, sensible tennis shoes, and bright jackets—exited the gallery and wandered away to explore more of the Seventh Arrondissement, the woman abandoned the boutique and quickly crossed the narrow Rue André to the arched doorway under five stories of iron balconies.

It was close to seven in the evening, and the woman interrupted the owner on his way to lock the door. A rotund man in his late forties with circular glasses and thinning dark hair combed straight back from his high forehead, he stepped back and waved her inside the shop, which contained paintings, bronze sculptures, furniture, and rugs as well as antique jewelry and snuffboxes. “Bonjour, Mademoiselle.”

“Bonjour.” She smiled apologetically and asked if he spoke English, even though she knew the answer.

“Of course. I am Henri Masard, the owner. How may I help you?”

“I have a painting I’d like to sell. A friend recommended you.” She pulled out a folded magazine page from her heavy leather handbag. He reached to take it, but she didn’t release it. “It requires discretion.”

He tilted his head in a small bow. “I understand. I can assure you, all transactions are completely private.”

She released the paper. He opened it, and the glossy paper reflected the light from a nearby lamp onto his glasses. He adjusted the glasses, and the opaque reflection disappeared, revealing a sharp gaze. After a quick glance at the paper, he looked at her, eyebrows raised.

“It’s true,” she said. “I have it.”

He locked the front door then refolded the paper. “May I?” he asked, gesturing to the interior pocket of his charcoal gray suit.

“Yes, keep it.”

“Let’s discuss this in my office.” He led the way to the back of the shop. They passed through an archway to a work area where a young woman with wheat-colored hair and a bright scarf bent over a table wrapping a vase. The man picked up several envelopes and spoke to her in French. She took the envelopes, reached for her purse, and headed for the front door.

He crossed to a wrought-iron spiral staircase in the back corner. “This way,” he said over the noise of his footsteps ringing on the iron. “My retreat.” He walked into a room with a large worktable positioned in front of a kitchenette. A heavy wooden desk sat on the other side of the room along with an ornately carved armoire, several file cabinets, and two chairs that were angled toward a small fireplace.

"Now," the man said as he gestured to one of the cracked leather chairs, "what shall I call you?"

"Zoe Hunter."

Half an hour later, the woman with the red hair left the gallery, took a taxi to Orly, and went directly to a restroom where she locked herself in a stall. She removed the red wig and shook out her black, chin-length asymmetrical bob. She stuffed the wig in her Gucci bag and left the restroom, her phone pressed to her ear as she headed for the gate where her departing flight to Naples was boarding. "He's in. He's making inquiries."

Four days later, Dallas

ZOE entered the kitchen, scrubbing her hand across her eyes and gave a visible start at the man pouring coffee into two mugs. "Jack Andrews, here in my kitchen. Still surprises me every time." She accepted the mug he held out.

"You wound me." He leaned back against the counter and took a sip from his own mug. "Am I so uninteresting that you're not even aware I'm here?"

"Oh, I'm aware, all right." Hard not to be aware of him with his dark slightly wavy hair and silvery blue eyes that took on an even deeper hue because of the cobalt dress shirt he wore. His gray dress pants and a yellow tie were at odds with his bare feet. Altogether, very hard to miss.

Jack raised an eyebrow, and Zoe buried her nose in her coffee. He had made it strong and black, just the way she liked it, and she needed that jolt of caffeine to make sure any other inanely revealing remarks didn't slip out. She pulled the cream cheese tub from the refrigerator and grabbed the package of bagels from the pantry on her way to the central island.

"So it's more that you expect me to disappear again without a word?" he asked.

"It has crossed my mind."

"Not going to happen." There was a conviction, a firmness to his tone that made Zoe look up from the cream cheese she was slathering across her everything bagel.

"Really?" Her eyes narrowed. "No flitting off to chase mysterious gunmen or pursue crime bosses around the world?"

"Not to point fingers, but you seem to do a lot of flitting around the globe yourself with only the slightest provocation."

"Slight provocation? You call FBI investigations and people trying to kidnap me, slight provocations?"

Jack waved his mug. "Completely understandable. I'm just pointing out that I'm not the only one setting off on globetrotting adventures. And, don't forget that I took myself out of the picture here to protect you."

"Pity that the people with guns didn't know that."

Jack turned and rummaged under the cabinet. "You're not fooling me." His voice was muted. "I know you better now. Granted, I'm not the fastest learner, but I do detect a pattern. I think I'm beginning to understand why you go on the defensive." Jack emerged with a skillet. "You're scared. Eggs?"

"I'm not scared."

"Not normally. Nothing seems to faze you—twenty foot-climbing walls or massive rollercoasters. But you might as well admit it. You find this," he pointed the skillet back and forth between them, "uncomfortable. You're scared of what it might mean. Under all that defensive snarkiness, you kind of like it that I'm back. And that, my dear, frightens you."

Zoe thumped her mug down on the counter. "Of all the conceited, smug, arrogant statements—"

"But is it true?"

"No, it's *not* true. I couldn't care less that you're back."

"Of course," he said mildly and turned his back as he put the skillet on a burner. "I'll get my coffee pot back from the FBI then you can have the kitchen to yourself again," he said over his shoulder. "I'll look for my own place."

Jack and Zoe had a complicated history. They'd married on impulse and dove into life as man and wife, buying a house almost before the ink was dry on the marriage certificate. Unfortunately, everyday life had turned out to be not quite happily ever after—so much so that they'd divorced, but by then the housing market bubble had burst, and they were saddled with a house no one wanted to buy. Neither of them could afford to take a loss, so they'd divided the house into his-and-hers territories with boundaries enforced as strictly as any iron-curtain state had guarded its frontiers pre-glasnost.

Zoe blew out a breath. "I'm sorry. You know I'm not...at my best before my second cup of coffee...and you..." *Look so damn good standing there in your bare feet*, she thought. Zoe gulped her coffee and burned her tongue. To drown out the words in her head, she said, "You're so wide-awake...and cheerful. It's annoying. No one should be cheerful before eight a.m."

"Noted. Gloomy disposition preferred in the a.m."

Zoe felt a smile tug at her mouth as she downed another gulp of coffee. "I am glad you're back," she allowed. "There's no need to talk about going back to the way we did things before. For one thing, you're not getting your coffee pot back from the FBI evidence locker—probably for another year or two." Zoe took another bagel from the bag and popped it in the toaster.

Jack cracked several eggs into the pan. "The turnaround on the FBI investigation does seem to move at the speed of a glacier. You'd have thought it would be closed by now, considering they're not charging me with anything, and they have all their answers."

"I've given up trying to understand the FBI. As long as they don't show up here with questions that I don't know the answers to, it's a good day."

Jack nodded as he added chopped ham and shredded cheese to the skillet.

"The other thing is that this is your house, too," Zoe continued. "You own half of it. We should be able to figure out how to live here together. I mean, not together *together*, but in the same house, sharing the same space. Surely, we're mature enough to share a kitchen. This is just an awkward stage." The bagel popped up in the toaster slot.

"You make us sound like we're in the adult equivalent of the terrible twos." He deposited the omelet onto a plate, handed it to Zoe, then turned back to make a second one for himself. Zoe spread some cream cheese on the toasted bagel and put it on Jack's plate as he said, "But you do have a point. I'm afraid moving out would present a few difficulties for me, considering my lack of employment."

"No word on the applications you have out?" Zoe asked as she dug into the omelet. Trust Jack to know how to make the perfect omelet. He was like that—dependable, knowledgeable, resourceful. He knew how to hang drywall, how to navigate to an address without using a GPS, and how to iron a dress shirt. He could probably even hem Zoe's new pants. She'd tried and now had pants that trailed an inch longer in the back than the front.

"Not much demand for an ex-spy turned failed entrepreneur with a gap year on his résumé." Since Jack's return to the United States, he had spent his time alternating between completing home repairs and sending out résumés. He sat down across from her at the island.

"Something will turn up." Zoe refilled her coffee cup. She raised her eyebrows and lifted the coffee pot. He waved her off with his fork. She returned to the island, and they ate in silence. The coffee had made its way into her system, and the casual intimacy of their situation hit her. Jack glanced up at her as he took a sip of his orange juice, the muscles of his throat working as he swallowed. She became aware she was only wearing her stripy pajama top and shorts. She felt her cheeks flush—her red hair and fair skin meant it wasn't easy to hide her reactions.

She cleared her throat and concentrated on her plate. "Why the suit?" The jacket was draped over the back of one of the barstools.

He'd been appearing downstairs in T-shirts and jeans while he repaired the gaping hole in the drywall in the kitchen ceiling, a reminder of a plumbing disaster that her meager savings account had only recently been able to cover.

"Job fair downtown. What's on your agenda today?"

"Three dogs to walk, lunch with Helen at the mall, then I have to drop off real estate flyers at a client's house." Zoe specialized in being a "Jill of all trades" and took on a variety of work to make ends meet. Most of her income came from two sources, the office suites her aunt had given her as an early inheritance, which she rented out, and the freelance copy-editing she did for *Smart Travel* guidebooks. Right now, she was between guidebooks and was picking up every odd job she could find.

With his elbows propped on the table, Jack cradled his mug in his hands. He gazed at her over the rim. "Zoe, would you like to go to dinner with me?"

"Of course, I'll eat dinner with you tonight." Zoe finished off the last bite of egg then said, "We've been eating dinner together for the last week."

"Not here. Would you like to go out to dinner? On a date."

"A date?"

He leaned closer. "It's part of my strategy. I'm going to woo you."

"Woo me?"

"Court you, whatever you want to call it."

"Why would you want to do that?"

"We messed things up a bit—rushed into a situation that neither of us was ready for. I'd like to try again, but in a different way. Take things slower." He put down his mug, picked up her empty plate, and stacked it on his.

She reached for the plate. "I can do that."

"I'll get it." He turned on the hot water and added a shot of dishwashing liquid to the rising water. "Need to earn my keep." He unbuttoned his cuffs and rolled up his sleeves to the elbows, exposing strong, tanned forearms.

"You didn't answer my question."

Zoe realized she was staring at his arms. "Umm—what?"

"Dinner?"

"Sure," she muttered and fled the kitchen.

ZOE stopped in front of a poster taped to the window of the Run-Bike-Swim store. "Look, the Tough Mudder is coming up. Let's do it."

"What's a Tough Mother?" Helen asked.

"*Mudder*. Tough Mudder. It's an adventure race with obstacles and challenges."

Helen frowned at the poster. "Why would I want to crawl through mud, climb huge walls, and," her eyebrows shot up under her golden bangs, "get an electric shock? People actually *pay* money to do this?"

"Yes. Come on, it will be a blast. Think how good you'll feel when we finish. What a sense of accomplishment you'll have."

Helen gave her a pitying glance. "I don't need an electric shock to feel accomplished. I'll just clean house. Ask Jack. He'd probably love it."

"I don't know if that's such a good idea."

"Why?" Helen asked.

Zoe recounted the conversation Jack and she'd had that morning. By the time she'd finished, they were in the mall's bookstore. "I was staring at his arms, watching his forearm muscles flex like some love-sick tween," Zoe said, her head turned sideways as she read the titles on the shelf under the DATING AND RELATIONSHIPS sign.

"So, he had nice forearms?" Helen asked.

"Tanned and taut and—" she broke off as she looked up and caught Helen's amused expression. "Go ahead. Laugh at me. I know it sounds stupid. I can't believe I'm saying it, either. I'd just never noticed what nice, strong arms he has."

"Yes, I'm sure when you were married you were too busy noticing other parts of him to admire his arms."

Zoe turned back to the shelves. "And what's up with this

wooing thing? Why would he want to do that? And what does that mean anyway? What kind of word is that, *woo*?"

"An old-fashioned word." Helen disappeared around the end of the aisle then returned with a dictionary. She put her raspberry smoothie on a shelf and opened the book. "Here it is. *To persuade, to court, to entice.* Sounds pretty good to me." She shut the book. "And you say he was doing the dishes at the time he mentioned wooing? I'd grab that man and hang on to him. Tucker hates to do dishes."

Zoe rolled her eyes. "This is a phase. Jack and I have already been through this. I'm not making the same mistake again." She went back to studying the spines. "Plenty of books on love languages and communication." Zoe ran her finger along the bookshelf. "But nothing on how to deal with an ex who comes back into your life after a year of dodging the FBI and Interpol for crimes he didn't commit."

"It's not exactly a common problem. Maybe you should try the romance section." Helen waggled her eyebrows.

Zoe pulled out a book, replaced it. "What brought on this change of heart?"

Helen sipped her smoothie and shrugged. "I'll admit I wasn't his biggest fan."

Zoe snorted.

Helen ignored her. "But it turns out, he had his reasons for doing what he did."

"Which part do you think I should overlook? Lying to me? Omitting huge chunks of his personal history, not to mention skipping town without a word, then staying in hiding for months on end?"

Helen's nose squished up. "I'll admit, it doesn't sound good when you put it like that. But he'd thought that he'd finally put that part of his life behind him. Also, he'd signed one of those confidentiality agreements—"

"I don't want to hear about confidentiality. You marry someone, you should tell them about your past, especially if it involves shady characters who want to mess with your current life."

"Did you tell Jack every detail about your past?" Zoe drew a breath to speak, but Helen kept talking. "About your mom? About the reality show?"

Zoe closed her mouth.

"I didn't think so," Helen said.

"He found out soon enough."

"Yes, but it's not fair to hold the full disclosure thing against Jack when you didn't fill him in on your history. Listen, I asked Tucker about those confidentiality agreements, and he said the government doesn't mess around. They're serious about tracking down people who talk about....well, about whatever they're not supposed to talk about. Anyway, the point is once all hell broke loose, Jack tried to keep you safe. And, despite everything that has gone on, look at you." Helen swept her smoothie cup down to Zoe's sandals. "Everything turned out okay. You're home, alive and unhurt. And it seems your FBI escort has disappeared, right?" Helen glanced around the bookstore. "I don't see that rumpled older guy or the hot younger one."

"You seriously think I should just forget all the lies, the deception?"

Helen sipped her smoothie for a moment. "You want to know what I really think?"

"Yes."

"Honestly?"

"Yes, although now I'm a little scared."

Helen guzzled more of her smoothie. "You know what, I shouldn't say. I shouldn't interfere." She focused on the titles. "You do what you think is right for you."

"Okay, now you have to tell me."

Helen sighed. "Don't be hasty. That's my advice."

"I need more than that."

"I realize getting back together with Jack goes against the grain for you, but I think you shouldn't turn him down without really thinking about it."

"What do you mean, goes against the grain?"

"Well," Helen raised a shoulder, "You keep most people at arm's length and following through is not exactly your strong point." Zoe opened her mouth, but Helen lowered her chin and talked over her. "The leaf biology project our freshman year. Remember?"

"Ugh. I'll never forget it. I still have nightmares about it, that I didn't get it finished." She sighed. "And you're right; the only reason I got the assignment turned in was because you were my partner."

"Don't feel too bad. That project was never ending. All those scientific names. I'm a detail person, and that one about did me in."

Zoe wanted to say she'd changed, but thought of her extremely long list of client follow-up calls that she never got around to making. "Okay, so following through is not my thing."

"Don't be too hard on yourself. The flip side of that is that you're flexible and spontaneous and decisive. Where I'd dither for days, you make the call, and go on. Anyway, all I'm saying is don't dismiss Jack without *really* considering what you're giving up. Despite everything that's happened, guys like him don't come along every day. Okay, stepping off my soapbox now. There's a book I want to find. I'll be over there." She walked away noisily slurping the dregs of her smoothie.

Zoe blew out a breath and shook her head. She knew Helen meant well, but there was no way Zoe was going to jump back into a relationship with Jack. She *had* thought about it. A lot.

She'd considered the possibility of getting back together with Jack, especially during their recent impromptu jaunts around Europe, but that wasn't real life. Sure, they'd connected, and she felt a tug toward him as if an invisible cord were pulling them together, but things were different here in the everyday, mundane world. Those experiences and emotions they'd shared were heightened. Fear and terror had a tendency to do that.

They did well as a couple under pressure, but she knew how they functioned in the real world. They'd been there, done that, and had a divorce certificate to show for it. Couldn't they transition to one of those cool divorced couples who got along better as friends than they ever did as husband and wife?

Since there didn't seem to be any how-to books on being a cool divorced couple, Zoe went to find Helen. She spotted her golden blond head under the PREGNANCY sign and hurried over, feeling like a heel. Had her moaning about her situation run over some big news from Helen?

"Find what you're looking for?" Zoe asked.

"Yep." Helen held up two books, *Everything You Wanted To Know About Infertility But Were Afraid to Ask* and *Eat Your Way Fertile*. "Apparently, I shouldn't have had that smoothie," she said, going for a light tone, but Zoe could sense the sadness laced within her words.

"Oh, Helen." Zoe gave her a one-armed hug. "Are you

sure you need...." she pointed to the books, "you've only been trying for a couple of months, right?"

She returned Zoe's hug then stepped away and squared her shoulders. "After ten months, I think it's time to admit that there *might* be a problem. Come on, let's check out. I want a burger, and I think I better eat it before I read this book."

LUCINDA McDaniel was a seriously successful Dallas realtor. She lived in a gated community, but since that apparently wasn't enough security, she had a set of gates at the foot of her driveway as well, which were set between tall stucco walls covered with tendrils of ivy.

Zoe's window on her old Jetta labored down, letting in a blast of warm air. Only March and it was already eighty-five and humid. She leaned out, punched in the code, and the gates began their slow crawl backward. Zoe accelerated between them when they were partway open, her mirrors coming within an inch of the iron. She navigated the gently rising curve of the drive through the lush landscaping quickly and then hit the brakes, parking dead center in the sweep of the driveway in front of the French-style home with a mansard roof and a mix of light stone, stucco, and decorative copper accents.

She grabbed the three stacks of papers she'd picked up at Staples and trotted up the steps. It was two-thirty on the dot. Lucinda disliked tardiness. The first time Zoe had met her, Lucinda had been chewing out her twentyish assistant for arriving with her Starbucks coffee at 9:02 instead of nine.

Lucinda sold luxury homes, and she wanted full-color

flyers that showed off every aspect of the high-end homes. Zoe was extremely happy that Lucinda was so busy with her clients that she didn't have time to layout, proof, and print the flyers herself. While there wasn't a salary high enough to entice Zoe to work with Lucinda one-on-one—Lucinda had a tiny employee retention problem—Zoe didn't mind working as a freelancer. Not one of her assistants had stayed over two months, so Zoe was happy to step in—for a nominal fee—and work with her virtually, which freed up Lucinda to meet with bigwig clients who wanted a mini-Versailles as their home sweet home.

A yellow post-it note on the front door handle stopped her from ringing the bell. "Out back. Gate to the left," it read.

Zoe retraced her steps back to the driveway then took the curving stone path to a metal gate with so many intricate curly-cues it looked like something out of a Tim Burton movie. She pushed it open. "Lucinda, it's me, Zoe."

The mechanical whir of an air conditioner hummed in the distance, and the wind filtered through the tall cottonwood trees shading the yard. "Lucinda?" she called again, scanning the large deck that dropped down to a brick terrace, which stretched to the pool's edge. The water glistened turquoise, reflecting back little sparks of sunlight.

Maybe Lucinda had gone inside? She shaded her eyes, checking each grouping of outdoor furniture scattered across the deck and terrace. She spotted a yellow legal pad with several pages curled back and a cell phone on a table next to a wicker chaise lounge, which was facing the pool, its back turned toward her.

"There you are," Zoe said.

Zoe covered the distance quietly. She could just see a wisp of Lucinda's black hair near the arm of the chair. Had

Lucinda curled up and fallen asleep? That would be a first. Zoe had never seen her when she wasn't moving. Maybe her hectic pace had finally caught up with her, and she was taking a short siesta. If she had, Zoe wouldn't wake her. She'd just leave the flyers.

Zoe stepped around the table, caught sight of Lucinda, and sucked in her breath. Lucinda was indeed sprawled on the chaise lounge, but she wasn't napping. She had a knife in her back.

2

Zoe jerked back, wanting to pull her gaze away from the knife handle, but she couldn't stop staring as the thought that Lucinda McDaniel was slumped over the arm of the chaise lounge with a knife sticking out of her back reverberated through her mind. On another level, Zoe registered in a distracted way that she had dropped the flyers. Most of them were at her feet, but the wind caught a few and whipped them toward the pool. Lucinda was going to be very upset.

Zoe gave herself a mental shake. What was she thinking? At this point, Lucinda had much worse problems than ruined flyers.

How had this happened? And was she...dead? Lucinda wasn't moving, but there wasn't much blood, just a splotch or two on the taupe and black striped cushion. Zoe wanted to step backward and run, but she had to check...see if there was anything she could do to help. She stepped over the flyers and squatted down so she could see Lucinda's face, which was pressed against the arm of the chair.

Her eyes were fixed and staring. Zoe stumbled backward, shocked at the vacant gaze. There was nothing she could do.

That was the last full thought she had before a sharp pain cracked into the back of her head, and the ground, covered with full-color pictures of pools and granite countertops, came rushing up to her.

THE first thing to penetrate the blackness was music. Music? What was going on? Zoe opened her eyes and blinding light cut across her pupils. Reflexively, she squished her eyes closed and groaned. Her head ached with a throb that seemed to go down to her spine. She hadn't felt this bad since the morning after Helen's bachelorette party.

Zoe narrowed her eyes and located the music. It was coming from the car radio, which was cranked up, pumping out Maroon 5's *Love Somebody*.

Radio? She was in...her *car*? She sat up. A wave of nausea hit her. She fought it down, working deep breaths in and out as she gripped the worn seat cover. She reached out a shaky hand and snapped off the radio. Cool air from the air conditioner flowed into the car, and she aimed one of the vents at her face, cautiously leaning forward. The seasick feeling was still there, but this time it was a ripple instead of a wave.

She looked out the window and saw the sun was lower, slanting directly into the Jetta's front window. The clock on the dashboard read three o'clock. She'd been out for a half-hour?

She looked from the clock to the imposing gates at the foot of Lucinda's drive. Lucinda. The knife. The blackness. Zoe put a tentative hand to the back of her head and felt a squishy bump. Someone had hit her....and carried her back to her car then kindly turned on the A/C so she wouldn't get too hot?

With a lunge that sent more shock waves through her head, Zoe hit the automatic lock button then reached into her messenger bag, which was in the passenger seat. Swallowing hard, she dug around until her fingers closed on her cell phone. Murmuring, "Thank God," Zoe dialed 911 and quickly shifted through the rest of the contents of her bag. Her wallet, a meager stack of single dollar bills, and her two credit cards were all there.

A woman's voice came on the line. "What is your emergency?"

"Lucinda McDaniel. She's dead. I'm at her house. I found her. With a knife in her back."

THE responding officer, Officer Alverez, took down Zoe's information and listened as she explained how she'd found Lucinda. "Then someone hit me on the head. That's all I know."

Officer Alverez's dark brown eyes looked concerned. "There's an ambulance on the way. Let's have them take a look at you when they get here."

A second police car rolled to a stop behind Alverez's vehicle and another police officer, a woman with her hair in a bun at the back of her neck, got out. While the two officers conferred, the ambulance arrived. Alverez directed the EMTs in Zoe's direction then he and the female officer approached the gates. He punched in the code Zoe had given him, the gates opened, and the police officers walked slowly up the drive, guns drawn and pointed at the sky.

Zoe had lights flashed in her eyes and the back of her head examined. "Any nausea?"

"Some when I first woke up, but not now."

"Blurred vision?"

"No."

He handed Zoe an ice pack. "Put that on your head for twenty minutes, and then take a break. A doctor should check you, and you shouldn't drive. We'll take you to the hospital. You can call someone to pick you up—"

Officer Alverez came through the gates, his stride quick. He pulled the EMT away for a quick chat that included several sidelong glances at Zoe then he approached her. "Mrs. Hunter, can you show me exactly where you found Lucinda McDaniel?"

"Yes." Zoe stood and waved off the EMT who was saying something about she didn't have to go. As they walked up the driveway, Officer Alverez said, "You said there was a note on the door to go around back?"

"Yes, on the handle."

"Did you leave it there?"

"Yes." They came to the front of the house, and Zoe could see there was no yellow square of paper stuck to the handle. She frowned. "The wind must have blown it away."

Officer Alverez asked, "Which way did you go from here?"

"Around this way. I couldn't find her at first, but then I saw the legal pad." Zoe followed the path through to the gate with the iron curly-cues into the backyard. She faltered to a stop. "Where are the flyers?" She scanned the pristine terrace and deck.

"What flyers?"

"The real estate flyers. That's why I was here, to drop off the flyers. When I saw the knife, I dropped them. They went everywhere."

Zoe darted forward, the sudden movement making her head pound. The legal pad and cell phone were gone. The chaise lounge was empty. Zoe spun to Officer Alverez, her stomach surging threateningly. "Where is she?"

"That's what we were hoping you could tell us."

"She was right there." Zoe pointed at the chaise. "She was slumped over the arm of the chair with a knife sticking out of her back. There was blood." Zoe ran her hand over the cushion, but it was dry. She flicked it up, checked the other side, but it was pristine, too.

Zoe felt her equilibrium go. Alverez grabbed her elbow and guided her to a chair. Zoe put her head in her hands. What had happened? Nothing made sense. A pair of dark shoes crossed in front of her, and she realized it was the female officer, speaking in low tones with Alverez. Zoe caught the words "head injury" as she looked up and saw both officers glance at her. They moved away a step, but Zoe still heard, "...not home...out of town."

"But she was here," Zoe said. "Right there, on that chaise lounge."

The female officer turned to her. "I spoke to her office. Lucinda McDaniel left yesterday for a vacation in Lake Tahoe."

"Well, they're wrong," Zoe said, the skepticism in the woman's tone making Zoe's words sharp. "She was here an hour ago." Zoe looked at Alverez and grimaced as she said, "She was dead, but she was here."

"So what are you suggesting happened?" the female officer asked. "That someone murdered Lucinda McDaniel, conked you on the head, then carried you out to your car and came back here to move the body?"

"I'll admit it sounds unbelievable, but what other explanation is there?"

The female officer stepped closer. "I don't think you understand what could happen to you. Do you realize we can charge you with making a false report?"

Alverez raised his hand. "Go easy, Smithson. No one is going to be charged with anything until we verify that Lucinda McDaniel is actually at Lake Tahoe." The female officer's lips pressed into a flat line, and her eyes narrowed. "I'm on it." She walked quickly away, and Zoe had the feeling Smithson would move heaven and earth to prove Zoe was wrong. Alverez continued, "In the meantime, after we've gone over everything, you should go to the hospital, get a written medical diagnosis of your injury."

"In other words, get it down in an official document that I have a head injury."

"Those are your words, not mine." He pulled a small notebook from his pocket. "But it couldn't hurt to hang onto your discharge paperwork."

ZOE walked Alverez through what happened—and it wasn't a single linear journey. No, they had to hang out on several points, including how long Zoe had worked with Lucinda, and why Zoe was at Lucinda's house in the first place. But those questions were nothing compared to the details Alverez wanted on where Lucinda's body had been and what she'd looked like. After crisscrossing through her story multiple times, Alverez waved the EMT over. Before Zoe was escorted to the ambulance, she saw the employee from McDaniel Realtors, who had arrived with a key to the house, emerge onto the back deck with Officer Smithson. "Not inside," Smithson said. The grounds had also been searched while Alverez questioned her. They didn't find Lucinda, a large knife, or even a speck of blood.

On the way to the hospital, Zoe called Helen. "Are you busy? Do you think you could get off work a little early?"

"Already did. I'm looking for yams."

Zoe blinked. Maybe she really was losing her grip on reality? "Did you say yams?"

"Yes. Wild ones. They might possibly increase my fertility, so I figured it couldn't hurt to try them."

"Oh."

"Why? What's going on?"

"I'm in an ambulance on the way to the hospital—I'm fine. It's only a precaution," Zoe said quickly. Helen in mother-hen mode was quite bossy.

"Oh my God. What happened?"

"I found Lucinda McDaniel with a knife in her back then someone knocked me out. Can you come pick me up?"

After a beat of silence, Helen said, "Of course."

3

Zoe felt like she'd been tucked away behind a curtained alcove around the hospital bed for hours. The curtains fluttered, and she expected to see Helen stepping into the bay in the ER. But it wasn't Helen.

"Jack. What are you doing here?"

"Helen called me. Sorry I missed your call earlier. Are you okay? What did the doctor say?" He was frowning, scanning her from head to toe.

"That I'm fine," Zoe said, distractedly, her thoughts racing back over the crazy afternoon. She'd called Jack? When? "Don't look so worried. It's only a little bump. No big deal."

"How do they know that?"

"They did a scan. I'm fine. Really."

"Should you be standing up?"

"Yes. I should. I'm going to find the nurse with my discharge paperwork so I can get out of here."

"I'm sure they'll be along in a moment. Why don't you at least sit down on the edge of the bed?" He took her arm and tried to move her backward.

She pulled away. "I'm *fine*. I just want to get out of this place."

Jack scanned her face, his head tilted to the side. "Don't like hospitals?"

"Let's just say I feel the same way about them as you do about heights." Zoe had recently discovered that Jack hated heights, or as he'd said, he hated the thought of *falling* from heights.

He handed her the ice pack she'd left on the bed. "You stay put. I'll take care of it."

Helen swept into the room. "Okay. I've got your after-care sheet." Jack nodded to her on his way out.

"Where's he going?" Helen asked.

"Supposedly, to get me out of here, if he can find a nurse. They seem to have disappeared."

"Oh, I have a feeling he won't have any trouble getting some attention at the nurses' station. Here's your phone and messenger bag." Helen had arrived at the ER shortly after Zoe, and Zoe had handed all her personal belongings off to Helen.

"You called him?" Zoe asked. "Why would you do that?"

"Because you did, it's in your call list. You called him before you called me. I figured you wanted him to know you were here."

Zoe frowned at her phone as she checked the list. "I called *Jack*? First, before anyone else? Even before I called you?"

Then it came back to her like a fuzzy dream that didn't make sense in the daylight. In the car, after she'd called 911, she had dialed Jack's number, but he hadn't answered.

"Interesting, isn't it?" Helen raised her eyebrows and

nodded her head in a knowing way. "What does that say? When you needed help, you called him."

The same thought was reverberating through Zoe's mind. Was she coming to...*depend* on Jack? No. That would never do. "It proves I was disoriented and confused," Zoe said briskly. "Did you tell him about Lucinda?"

"Only that you'd found her. He said he'd get here as soon as he could."

Zoe transferred the ice pack from one hand to another and rubbed her forehead. She hadn't told Helen that Lucinda's body was missing. The more she thought about the whole situation, the crazier it made her sound. Now that she was away from Lucinda's house, the entire afternoon seemed like a strange hallucination.

Jack reentered the room with a nurse. Once Zoe signed the forms, they made their way to the parking lot where Helen and Jack decided that Jack would drive Zoe home, and Helen would coordinate with Tucker so they could pick up Zoe's car and drop it off at her house after Tucker got off work.

"Excuse me, but don't I get a say in any of this?" The sun hovered at the horizon, but the brightness of it made her pulse throb in her head. Zoe found her sunglasses and slipped them on. "I'm standing right here. Helen can drop me off at my car. I'll drive it home."

"Nope." Helen tapped the paper. "No driving for you. Rest and ice. That's all that's on your agenda tonight." As Jack moved some paperwork out of the passenger seat of his car, Helen added, "Oh, and being woken every few hours tonight. I think that's Jack's department." She winked at Zoe then handed off the sheet with the after-care notes to Jack. She turned back to Zoe, all teasing gone from her tone. "What a horrible, horrible thing to happen. I'm so glad you're okay."

Zoe gave Helen a quick hug. "Thank you for meeting me here."

Helen patted Zoe on the arm. "Of course. Rest up and don't forget to ice that bump. Later, I want all the details about what happened. What a shock. I can't believe Lucinda McDaniel is dead."

"You don't know the half of it," Zoe murmured as she slid into the passenger seat and waved to Helen. The air in the car was scorching and thick with the fragrance of flowers.

"It smells great in here. Is that one of those air freshener things?" Zoe checked the rearview mirror for a dangling cutout of a flower, but there wasn't one. "I think I need one for my car."

"No, dang it, it's the real thing." Jack switched the air conditioner to high then reached in the back seat. "I forgot about these and left them in the car. They've wilted. Pity." He handed her a bundle of flowers wrapped in green tissue.

"Jack, these are gorgeous." The bouquet was a burst of color: delicate pink tulips, yellow snapdragons, deep blue hyacinths, orange mums, and tiny wild roses in red, white, and pink. "But you didn't have to get me flowers. I was only in the hospital for a few hours. Thank God."

Jack pulled into the traffic. "They were for our date."

"Our date? Oh, our *date*."

Jack kept his attention on the road. "Which I can see you were anticipating with baited breath."

"Sorry. With everything that's happened, I'd completely forgotten."

"Understandable." Jack sent her a quick smile before he

changed lanes. "A dead body and a blow to the head would override dinner plans."

"But these really are beautiful. I've never seen a bouquet like this before."

He lifted one shoulder. "A dozen red roses didn't seem like your style. Too trite. And boring."

Zoe fingered one of the petals. "I'd never turn down flowers of any kind, but you're right. I'm not exactly a hothouse flower kind of girl."

Jack stopped at a light then held her gaze. "No. You definitely need something more...exotic."

Zoe felt a blush spreading across her cheeks again. What was it with these blushes lately? The car behind them honked, and Jack slowly transferred his attention to the road. "So, dinner? Do you want something to eat?"

"Yes. I'm starving."

"How about Chinese? It's not the dinner I had planned, but..."

"Oh, egg rolls and sweet and sour chicken. Excellent idea. We can call in an order when we get home."

"Okay." Jack merged into traffic on the freeway. "So you want to tell me about the other half?"

"What?"

Jack glanced over his shoulder before changing lanes. "When Helen said she wanted all the details, you said she didn't know the half of it. What's the other half?"

"You're going to think I'm crazy." Zoe rubbed a hand down her jeans. "The police think I'm some sort of mental case."

"Try me."

She blew out a breath. Even she was beginning to doubt

what she'd seen. She'd been so sure of what happened when she first came to in the car, but the more time that passed, the more uncertainty crept in. How could Lucinda's body be there, then gone? It didn't make sense.

Could it have been some elaborate trick? But who would play a trick like that? She could almost see it being part of a prank reality show and, normally, she wouldn't put anything past her mom, who had been the driving force behind her family's appearance on a reality show when Zoe was in her tweens. But Donna had a steady gig as a retirement lifestyle correspondent for a morning show with a major network now. The producers were strict about what Donna could and couldn't do—appearances and promotions—and Zoe was pretty sure that the producers of the morning show would nix any idea of Donna pranking someone with a dead body or being involved with a show that did that.

"Zoe?"

Zoe shook her head. "It seems surreal now. Unbelievable."

"I've had some unbelievable experiences myself, and they were true. It can't be worse than someone taking out a hit on you. That's not exactly common."

"It's worse. Lucinda's body is gone." Zoe cringed as she said it. It sounded even more absurd when she said it aloud. The evening rush-hour traffic swished around them, all those normal people hurrying to get home and fix dinner or get the kids to soccer practice.

"What do you mean gone?"

"Gone. Disappeared. Not there. Taken. I don't know. She was sprawled on the chaise lounge with a knife in her back. I was staring at her when I was hit on the head. I woke up in my car and called the police. When I led the police into the backyard, Lucinda's body was gone. Nowhere in the backyard or the house. Not even a drop of blood on the chaise cushions. I can tell the police think I'm either some odd person bent on getting attention, or someone who needs some medication."

Jack watched the traffic, smoothly shifting into the fast lane to pass a car, but Zoe could tell his thoughts were on what she'd said. "Hmm...Yes, that is bad. Not particularly worse than the hit man, but a definite tie." He shot her a quick smile before sliding into the exit lane, and she felt the knot of anxiety loosen a bit. He hadn't scoffed or written it off as a side effect of the head injury.

"So you believe me?"

"Of course."

"Why? I'm beginning to doubt it myself."

"Well, you're not a liar, you're not prone to psychotic breaks, and," he hesitated, his voice turning serious as he said, "because when I couldn't count on anyone else, you were there for me. The last thing I'm going to do is doubt you."

"That's overly generous. I only helped you because I'd been pulled in as deep as you and wanted answers."

"That was true in the beginning." He sent her a piercing look with those silvery blue eyes.

"Okay, I'll admit it. I did believe you, especially about the hit man. It wasn't exactly a leap of faith to believe when someone was taking potshots at you. This is totally different. There's no proof that I saw Lucinda. There's no proof that Lucinda was even there."

"Why do you fight me, on everything?" He grinned. "Let me believe you, if I want to. Go through everything that happened again for me, will you? I want to get it straight in my head."

Zoe blew out a breath. He was right. Why was she trying to talk him out of believing her? She should just be glad he did and go on.

By the time she'd recounted the series of events, they were turning into their subdivision, Vinewood. The sun had set, but the horizon still glowed orange in the twilight. Their neighborhood was established, and the mature cottonwood trees lining the street blocked out most of the dusky light. Zoe took off her sunglasses as she finished reciting what had happened.

Jack flicked on the headlights. "There's one thing that doesn't fit."

"Just one?"

"The flyers. You said you dropped them."

"Yes, they went everywhere."

"How many?"

"Ah, let's see. There were three houses, so three hundred. One hundred copies for each house."

"And they were gone when you went back in the yard?"

"I didn't see a single one."

"That's a lot of paper to disappear." Jack's mouth quirked down. "I wonder if the police checked Lucinda's trash?"

"I don't know. I'd assume they did. They looked everywhere for her, even under the deck. Hey, who's at our house?" They were still half a block away, but Zoe could see there were two pickups parked in front of their house. A long trailer was attached to one of the trucks.

"Looks like a yard service. Maybe for one of the neighbors?" Jack asked.

Zoe read the magnetic sign attached to the pickup's driver

door as they drove by. "I've never noticed Green Lawn Care around here before." Now that they were closer, Zoe saw a riding lawn mower, a small bobcat, and other lawn maintenance equipment like shovels, rakes, and edgers in the trailer.

A man in a lime-green shirt with the words GREEN LAWN on the pocket and straw hat with a wide brim came down their driveway, gave them a little two-finger salute, and climbed into the pickup with the trailer. By the time Jack parked the car beside the second pickup, which was in their driveway, the pickup with the trailer was already lumbering down the street.

Another man closed the gate to their backyard and came across the driveway toward them. He moved with a stiff-legged stride, rocking his shoulders from side to side in a way that reminded Zoe of a penguin. The fact that he wore black pants and had a stripe of a white dress shirt showing between the edges of his open black leather jacket only added to the impression. "Just finished up." He waddled toward them. "I think you'll be pleased with the new landscaping." His voice had a nasal quality and the quick cadence of his words indicated he was from another part of the country besides Texas.

"You must be at the wrong house," Zoe called. "I don't have any landscaping scheduled."

The man scratched his cheek and consulted a clipboard that had been tucked under his arm. "Zoe Hunter? Five-two-five-one Vinewood Avenue?" His thin salt and pepper hair must have once been shaped into a crew cut, but it had grown out several inches and spiked up above ruddy cheeks and watery brown eyes.

"This day just gets weirder and weirder," Zoe muttered to Jack. She tucked the flowers into the crook of her arm and reached out to take the clipboard the man held out. "There's got to be a mistake. I didn't—" she broke off as she looked at the clipboard.

One of Lucinda's flyers was pinned under the shiny metal clip. For a second Zoe couldn't say anything. A gust of wind flicked the edge of the paper back, revealing more identical flyers.

4

"Where did you get these?" Zoe demanded.

The man lifted his chin in the direction of the house. "Why don't we step inside and talk about it."

"No, I think we should call the police." Zoe turned to Jack. "These are the flyers that disappeared." She could tell Jack had picked up on the tension in her voice. If someone had given him a quick glance they wouldn't see anything different from a few moments earlier, but Zoe knew him well enough to recognize well-disguised wariness as he slowly circled the hood of the car.

"That is why it's important we talk." The man pulled back the edge of his jacket, revealing a handgun tucked into a holder at his hip.

Jack halted.

"Don't worry," the man said with a little laugh. "I don't want to use it. All I want to do is talk."

Zoe and Jack exchanged a glance.

He let the jacket fall back over the gun. "Just a simple

conversation, and then I'll leave. I promise, you want to hear what I have to say. Otherwise, I *will* contact the police."

"Let's do that now." Jack pulled his cell phone out of his pocket.

The man shrugged. "Fine by me, but I don't think you want her to go to jail, do you? Or, did I completely misjudge your feelings for her?"

Jack's finger hovered over the keypad.

"What are you talking about? I haven't done anything wrong." Zoe shook the clipboard at him. "I have nothing to be afraid of," she said, but she could feel blood pumping through her veins. A surge of nervousness hit her as she remembered the doubtful looks the police had sent her way this afternoon.

"You know that." The man extended his hands then brought them into his chest. "I know that. But it is a question of perception, isn't it? The police already think you to be...unbalanced. A few interesting details could push their opinion of you to seriously disturbed. And when there is evidence to support that view..." He trailed off then shrugged again. "Again, it doesn't matter to me. I simply want to talk." He held up his hands, palms out. "In fact, I will leave the gun in the truck, if it will make you feel better." Jack tensed as the man removed the gun from the holster, but he didn't seem to notice. He opened the door on the driver's side, shoved the gun under the seat, and slammed the door. He activated the lock with the key fob and turned back to them. "There. Now, surely we can talk."

Zoe swallowed. "Let's hear what he has to say."

Jack looked like he wanted to disagree.

"Excellent." The man headed for the front door.

Jack fell into step beside Zoe and said in a low voice, "Not a good idea."

"I don't love it either, but I want to know what information or...evidence...he has that he thinks he could take to the police."

"You know he could still be armed? He might have another gun—or something else—on him."

"I know, but I have you on my side. He's probably twice your age, not to mention that you're nearly twice his size. I think you can take him, if you have to."

"Oh, so now you're happy to have me on your side?"

"I'm always happy to have you on my side. Sometimes I just have trouble showing it."

The man had stepped to one side of the front door. Zoe juggled the clipboard and the flowers as she unlocked the front door. She noticed that Jack stayed back from the man, giving him a wide berth. Zoe led the way through the hallway and into the formal living room, snapping on lights as she went.

"What a lovely home."

Neither Zoe nor Jack answered him, but it didn't seem to bother him. He took one of the armchairs across from the couch, sprawling back with a sigh as if he was glad to be off his feet. Zoe put the flowers and the clipboard along with her messenger bag on one of the end tables then went to stand across from him, behind the couch, arms crossed. Jack stayed on his feet as well, moving to the side and slightly behind the man. "So what is this about?"

"I suppose I should introduce myself. I know you, but you do not know me. It is unfair for you to be at a disadvantage."

Zoe could see Jack practically grinding his teeth together. She didn't blame him. She wanted the guy to get on with it, too. "And you are?" she asked.

"Oscar. I work for Mr. Darius Gray."

He paused as if they should recognize the name. Zoe didn't. She looked at Jack, and he raised his shoulders in a slight shrug.

"I'm afraid we're not familiar with this Mr. Gray."

Oscar sighed. "I thought as much. Otherwise, why would you...well, I'm getting ahead of myself." He rearranged his body, sitting up straighter. "You have something that belongs to Mr. Gray. He wants it back."

"Ah, no, we don't. How could we have something that belongs to him when we don't even know him?"

"Let me be more specific. Mr. Gray wants you to return his painting. Now, I'm sure you didn't realize it was his because no one takes what belongs to Mr. Gray. He's giving you the opportunity to return it before he...takes action."

"He's accusing us of stealing," Jack said from the back corner.

Oscar swiveled to him. "Not stealing. At least, not intentionally. You saw an opportunity and took it. I'm sure you had no idea you were taking Mr. Gray's property. That is why he's willing to show some latitude."

"What is he going to do? Press charges?" Zoe rubbed her forehead. Her head was throbbing again, and she wished she'd taken the nurse's offer of pain medicine. "This conversation is absurd. He can talk to the police all he wants. We don't have any paintings, so we can't have one that belongs to Mr. Gray." Zoe gestured to the collage of snapshots she'd taken in London. "A few photos like those, but that's it. Our budget doesn't run to anything on canvas."

"You can protest all you like, but Mr. Gray knows you visited a dealer in Paris four days ago and inquired about selling the painting."

"Paris? That's crazy. I haven't even been outside Dallas for months."

The man's expression didn't change. "I wouldn't bother denying it. You're very memorable with your long red hair."

"But it wasn't me!"

"Like I said, you can deny it, if you want. Doesn't matter to me. No matter how discreet you thought you were, information can always be bought. If you look hard enough, there's usually someone who saw or overheard something. The shop assistant, a very attractive young lady, was very willing to provide your name and description once she realized she'd be amply—and discreetly—compensated.

"But—"

"Yes, I know. I know." He waved his hand in a circle. "You weren't there." He slapped his palms down on his thighs and prepared to stand. "That is of no importance now. All that matters is that Mr. Gray gets his painting back, seeing as how it's payment for services he's already rendered."

"What kind of services?" Jack asked.

"That's not what matters here. He knows you saw an opportunity in Germany and took the painting. He wants it back."

When he said the word *Germany*, everything clicked into place as if someone twisted a key in a lock and opened a door. Her gaze flew to Jack's face. She could see he remembered, too. Zoe swiveled back to Oscar, who was now standing.

"You've got the wrong person. Yes, we were there in Germany, at the castle, but we didn't take the painting. We saw who did, though. It was the woman who was there—the secretary. What was her name?" Zoe looked to Jack.

"Anna. Anna Whitmore, I believe."

"That's right." Zoe turned back to Oscar. "We saw her. She

came in the room where we were and switched contents of a leather carrying tube, which had been in the room, for the contents of a cardboard tube she'd brought with her. After the switch, she took the cardboard tube away with her." Zoe glanced back at Jack. "It must have been a painting. It wasn't stiff like a roll of paper. It was softer, with some flexibility, like canvas. She left with it. We have no idea where it is."

Jack nodded, but Oscar spread his hands. "This is a good yarn you've spun. Not bad, especially considering that you've come up with it on the spur of the moment, but it doesn't change the fact that you contacted Gallery Twenty-Seven about selling Marine."

He held up a hand as Zoe opened her mouth to speak. "Mr. Gray has also seen the financial transactions involving Verity Trustees. We all know that Mr. Costa purchased the painting, but, interestingly, he had the financial records altered so that your name is listed as owner of the company that paid the invoice for the twelve million dollars to buy the painting. Quite a merry little chase he put Mr. Gray's computer experts through, but, in the end, financial records show you bought it. I suppose you uncovered the set-up and took the painting, not realizing it was intended for Mr. Gray?"

Zoe felt lightheaded. "Twelve million dollars?" She never thought she'd dislike a number like twelve million dollars, but that was the amount of money that had gone missing from Jack's business account and set off a fraud investigation. She and Jack had found proof that neither one of them were involved in the financial slight-of-hand that made the money disappear, and last she'd heard, the FBI was running down all the accounts the money had been sifted through. Her heart-beat spun into high gear. What if this guy was right and the money trail did lead back to her? That sounded exactly like something Costa would do. Unsavory didn't begin to describe his character, and Zoe didn't doubt for a moment that he would set up a scheme to implicate someone else to hide his activities.

She closed her eyes briefly. Costa was dangerous and ruthless, but the FBI knew all about him now, and if he'd set up some sort of scheme to finger Zoe for using stolen money to buy a very expensive painting, wouldn't the FBI have come knocking on her door? They'd never been shy about asking questions before. "That can't be true. If it were, the FBI would be here, asking me about it."

Oscar snorted. "The FBI is bogged down. Budget cuts, you know. Their tech services division has been cut in half. Also, I believe higher priority cases keep bumping yours down the stack, so to speak. I'm sure they will get to it. Of course, if you help Mr. Gray, he would be willing to make sure all of Verity Trustees' transactions disappear. In fact, he could make it as if Verity Trustees never existed. Records can be lost..."

Oscar reached in a pocket of his leather jacket, and Jack tensed. "No need to be so jumpy." Oscar removed a business card and reached across the empty couch to hand it to Zoe.

A single phone number with a Dallas area code was centered on the heavy white cardstock.

Oscar took a few steps toward the hall. "You have three days. Mr. Gray understands that you probably have the Monet in free port in Geneva or Singapore and that it will take some time to retrieve it. Call that number when you have the painting in your possession. You will be informed where to bring it."

Zoe shot a desperate look at Jack. This guy would not listen to them.

Jack said, "You don't seem to understand. We *can't* do this for you. We don't have any idea were the painting is. We can't help you."

"Oh, I think you will."

"Those financial transactions will be disproved, once the FBI digs into them," Jack said, and Zoe knew he was saying it for her as much as he was to make a point to Oscar. Just hearing the words in his steady, reasonable tone made her feel better. "We've already proved to the FBI that we weren't involved in the fraud and that we didn't have access to the money. They'll know the transfers are faked."

Oscar's lips puckered as if he'd eaten something tart. "That could possibly be the case," he allowed. "But I think you will still help us."

"Why?" Zoe asked. Did this guy ever quit?

He looked toward the clipboard on the end table. "Because of Lucinda McDaniel."

The flyers. It seemed like it had been hours since she'd first caught sight of them on the clipboard. "What does this have to do with those flyers and with Lucinda?"

"Lucinda—or more precisely—her body is the incentive for you to give the painting to Mr. Gray."

"What? What are you talking about? Her body is missing."

"No. Her body is buried in your backyard under a new row of hedges along your privacy fence. They look quite nice."

"That's absurd," Zoe said, but inside she felt a curl of doubt as Oscar stared at her impassively.

"I assure you. It's true."

Lucinda was missing. The man had been in the backyard. There had been a backhoe on the trailer of the other truck. No one was home for several hours this afternoon...

Everything seemed to blur for a moment—Oscar's voice faded to an indistinct murmur, and the room went hazy. The walls seemed to curve around her. She braced her hand against the back of the couch.

Jack's voice cut through the murkiness. She felt his hand on her back. "Are you okay?"

She breathed deeply and the room settled back into its normal orientation.

Jack slipped a hand under her arm. "I'm not going to faint or anything, but I'm not okay if someone I know is buried in my backyard. How could that even happen? Someone would see you."

"Your six-foot privacy fence allowed us to work unobserved. Collecting the body unnoticed wasn't difficult at all. Once we put you in your car, we simply pulled into the driveway of Ms. McDaniel's home. A lawn maintenance crew is unremarkable. All we had to do was gather up the flyers and the bloody lounge cushion, zip everything into a body bag, place it in with the hedges, flowers, and bags of mulch in the trailer, and bring it here."

"So what about before? You killed her?" Zoe felt a warning pressure as Jack's hand tightened on her arm, but she had to ask.

Oscar shook his head. "No, that was my associate. I am a little slow for a job like that." He chuckled, and Zoe could only stare at him. He cleared his throat. "You see how it is now. You will collect the painting and call us. You are connected with Ms. McDaniel's death. You were at her house shortly before she died. You had an argument last week, and—"

"What? No. We never argued."

He shook his head, his expression pitying. "You really

don't understand how this works yet? One of the employees in McDaniel Realty overheard the argument and will be happy to speak to the police. Remember what I said about information being bought for the right price? It can be created, too."

"But that's not true," Zoe said.

Oscar continued as if she hadn't spoken. "Then there are the flyers, which have your fingerprints on them. The rest of them are buried with the body."

"Why are you doing this? You killed a woman for a *painting*?"

"We considered holding one of your friends, like Helen, or a relative—your Aunt Amanda or your mother—and demanding the painting as ransom." Zoe closed her eyes. This was a nightmare. This man knew everything about her.

"However, Mr. Gray believes individuals always work harder to rescue themselves than to rescue others, no matter how close the relationship. Saving your own skin is the highest motivator. And that is exactly what will happen if you bring us the painting."

"You're going to magically make Lucinda's body disappear from my yard?"

He frowned at her. "No. We will remove it in a way that draws no attention, insure it is found, and that there is no connection to you."

"What about her family, her friends, her business? You can't fix that."

"No." His phone beeped, and he reached inside his coat for it. He checked the display as he said, "Collateral damage is often unavoidable." He replaced his phone. "I really must go now. I'll see myself out."

5

"I can't quite believe it." Zoe and Jack stood side-by-side staring at the new hedge along the fence. "It just seems so bizarre. Should we...check?"

"I think we have to. I'll get a shovel." It was fully dark, and the porch light threw their giant sized shadows across the backyard.

While Jack was in the garage, Zoe edged up to the row of bushes as if there might be a rattlesnake in the woodchips. Jack returned and poised the shovel under the leaves of the first bush. He put his foot on the edge of the blade. "Ready?"

"Not really."

"You can wait inside."

"Are you kidding? This is my mess. I should be the one digging."

"Not your mess. Our mess." He shifted his weight, and the shovel sank into the ground smoothly. He transferred a scoop of earth and woodchips to the side and kept digging. "The soil is loose, like it's been turned recently."

Zoe nodded. Her throat felt dry. "I should get a flashlight," she said, but didn't move. Jack transferred several shovels of dirt and the bush tilted as the supporting earth was removed. Zoe pulled the bush to the side. The deeper he dug, the more carefully Jack maneuvered the shovel. About two feet down, he stopped. "I've hit something."

"Rock?"

"No." He probed the dirt gently with the shovel. "It's soft."

Zoe's stomach twisted. "Don't use the shovel." She kneeled down and reached to brush the dirt away.

"Don't use your hands." She looked over her shoulder at him. With the porch light behind him, he was a silhouette. "Fingerprints."

"Oh. Right. I'm not thinking clearly right now. Good thing I've got that whole head injury thing as an excuse. Let me get a spade or something." She sprinted to the garage and returned with some gardening tools and gloves.

She used a spade to carefully sweep away a layer of dirt, revealing thick plastic. It was a silver color and contrasted with the dark earth. With shaking hands she removed more of the dirt until she uncovered a zipper. She sat back. "It's true. That's a body bag."

Jack kneeled beside her.

"I can't do it." She swallowed hard. "I can't open it, but we have to. We have to see if...Lucinda is really in there. It could all be a joke, right? Just some crazy weirdo playing a trick on us."

"I'll open it." Jack pulled on one of the gardening gloves then inched the zipper open.

Zoe flinched backward at the smell, but not before she saw a tangle of dark hair and Lucinda's pale face.

ZOE turned off the faucet in the hall bath with trembling fingers and dabbed at her sweaty forehead with the hand towel. She'd been sick. She managed to lurch away from Lucinda's body to the other side of the yard before she threw up. She closed her eyes. Poor Lucinda. She wasn't what you'd call a sweet person—she was mean, actually—but she didn't deserve to be killed.

Zoe twisted the towel in her hands. Oscar hadn't lied about burying Lucinda. Did that mean what he'd said about the financial records tracing back to her name was true, too? What were they going to do?

The back door thudded closed, and Zoe hurried down the hall to the kitchen. Jack stood at the sink soaping his hands. "It's all back in place, the soil, the hedge, everything."

"What? Why did you do that? We've got to call the police."

He rinsed his hands. "We can't call the police, Zoe. Think about it. Lucinda is missing." He turned the faucet off and swiveled to face her. "You reported to the police that you'd seen her dead body today. If we call them and tell them her body is buried in our backyard, but we didn't put her there, do you think they'll believe us?"

She realized she still held the towel from the bathroom and gave it to him to dry his dripping hands. "Okay. Okay. You're right." Zoe paced around the island. "I get it, but we have to do something. We can't just leave her out there." She stopped. "Wait. Mort. We can call Mort."

"Agent Vazarri? Not a good idea."

Zoe raced into the formal living room where she'd left her messenger bag, located her phone, and dashed back to the kitchen. "He'll help us. He knows all about what happened before. He'll believe us. He's with the FBI. He can investigate this Darius Gray and figure out what's going on."

Zoe had been scrolling through her contact lists as she spoke. She found his name and dialed his cell phone. What did it say about the craziness of her life that she had an FBI agent in her contact list? He'd given her his card when he first began investigating the fraud case, and when she realized he might actually believe that she wasn't involved in scamming people out of money—that he was on her side—she'd saved his phone number.

"Zoe." Jack's voice had a warning tone. "Think about what you're doing. You could go to jail. Take it from someone who's been the focus of a criminal investigation, you don't want to do this. You're putting yourself at their mercy. I know you think he's nice, but he's going to err on the side of the law."

Zoe waved him off. A female voice answered. Probably his wife. "May I speak to Mort, please?"

"He's not available. Can I have him call you back?"

"Ah, can you get in touch with him? It's kind of an emergency."

"No, I'm afraid not. What's your name again?"

"Zoe. Zoe Hunter." Jack threw his gaze up to the ceiling and turned away from her. "It's related to an investigation. An old case."

"Oh, well, you'd better call the Bureau. Didn't you know? Mort's retired."

"No. I didn't know." Zoe took a deep breath. "Look, are you his wife? Because it's really important that I talk to Mort. It will only take a few minutes..."

"Wife? No, honey, I'm the house sitter. Mort and Kathy are on a Mediterranean cruise. I'll tell him you called next time he checks in. But it may not be for a while. They wanted a real vacation with no interruptions, so he had his calls from his cell phone forwarded to the house phone. I'm sure he'll get back to you."

Zoe ended the call. "Mort's on a cruise."

"Thank God. Zoe, there were real estate flyers in the bag with Lucinda's body. I saw them when I zipped the bag up."

Zoe put her hand over her mouth then whispered through her fingers, "My prints will be on them."

"You don't want to call that other agent, do you?"

"Sato? No. He never liked me. He'd have me locked up before Lucinda's body was even out of the ground. There's no one else we can go to. What are we going to do?"

They stared at each other for a moment.

She knew what he was thinking. "We have to find that painting, don't we?"

6

Zoe spun away from him, her hands pressed to her forehead. "But how? It's impossible. All we know is that some person with red hair used my name and offered to sell a painting to a gallery in Paris. We can't find the painting from that."

"He said it was a Monet."

"Even with that, there's got to be hundreds of Monet paintings."

"And he said the name of the gallery. Gallery Twenty-Seven." Jack grabbed a pencil and the magnetized notepad hanging on the refrigerator door. "Let's get everything, every little detail he said down on paper. He also mentioned the name of the painting."

Zoe leaned on the island beside him, latching onto the activity. Anything was better than helpless worrying. "I can't remember exactly. The whole conversation was surreal. I was so focused on making him understand we didn't have it, that I don't remember all the specifics. Wasn't it something...military?"

"Yes." Jack tapped the pencil against the paper several times. "Marine. That was it." Jack shot her a smile as he jotted it down. "What else?"

"Okay." Zoe studied the new drywall on her ceiling as she thought. "He talked about cities: Freeport, Geneva, and Singapore, but the way he said it...was weird. Something about us having the painting in Freeport, *in* Geneva or Singapore, which doesn't make any sense." She pushed away from the island and retrieved her new computer, which only took moments to bring up a browser.

While she typed, Jack added words to his list, reading them out. "He talked about the financial transactions, Verity Trustees, and the twelve million dollars."

Zoe's fingers paused. "That worries me. What if the FBI isn't finished investigating? What if Costa set me up? It would be just like him—use the money from the scam to buy world-class art and finger me as the culprit."

"I meant what I said. I don't think the FBI is going to buy a false trail like that, not after the way this whole case has gone. For all we know, the case is closed, and he just said that to scare you."

"He wasn't lying about anything else."

Jack reached for her hand. "Let's go one step at a time."

Zoe squeezed his hand. "Right. Find the painting. Simple. Easy," she said with a bogus, breezy tone that she didn't feel. "Mark that off our list, and *then* we'll worry about FBI investigations."

Jack leaned over and kissed her hard on the mouth. "You're lying through your teeth," he said, keeping his face close to hers. "But very brave."

She couldn't help smiling back at him. "Foolhardy, probably." He leaned forward and they kissed again, this time slowly, lingeringly.

Jack pulled away. "Much as I'd like to continue this, I don't think this an ideal time to get distracted."

Zoe felt as dizzy and as disoriented as she had when she had woken up in her car earlier that afternoon. How could that happen when only their lips had touched? She hadn't moved her arms to reach for him. Her fingers were still poised on the computer keypad. She cleared her throat, torn between not wanting to let on how much that kiss had rocked her and wanting to throw her arms around Jack. But she wasn't sure she could handle what would happen if she pulled him back to her, so she went with option A. "Right. Business before pleasure and all that." She scanned the search results and clicked through a few articles.

Jack sent her a look. "Don't tempt me."

"I thought you were wooing me. Is this wooing?"

"No. This is flirting, an essential part of wooing. Now, did you find anything?"

"Yes, I think so. Freeport is a city in the Bahamas, but when I combine it with Geneva, I get some interesting results. Freeport, either in a compound form or separate in two words, has another meaning, an economic free-trade zone."

"No taxes?"

"Exactly. There's a huge warehouse-type place in Geneva and one in Singapore, too, where collectors keep art and apparently lots of other things like gold bars, wine, even luxury cars." Zoe shook her head as she read through one of the articles. "Can you imagine? A warehouse full of tax-free luxury goods? It sounds like if you sell something on the premises, neither the seller nor the buyer pays taxes or custom duties. Listen to this line." She read aloud, "Free ports like the one in Geneva are ideal for art collectors who are not interested in displaying their art and need a secure storage location."

"Sounds like the go-to place for stolen art."

"Doesn't it?" Zoe sat back. "Of course, there's no way of knowing if the painting is there. I'm sure Mr. Gray—whoever he is—would use a place like this, but for all we know, Anna might have it under her bed." Zoe forced her thoughts away from all the thousands of possibilities of where the painting could be. She blew out a sigh. "This is why he gave us three days, for the travel time. So we could go and get it from Geneva or...wherever."

"Three days is a good thing."

"I hope it's enough. What's next?" Zoe asked, nodding at the list. She suddenly was very aware of the seconds ticking by.

"The painting and the gallery."

"Okay, *Marine*," Zoe said as she typed.

Jack pulled out his phone. "I'll search for the gallery. That shouldn't be too hard to run down."

Zoe frowned at the computer screen as she studied images of galleons and stormy seas. "Fifty-six million results for '*Marine* painting.' " She tried again, using the search term "*Marine* by Monet."

Jack said, "I've got the gallery. It's on the left bank, open Tuesday to Saturday. Owner is Henri Masard."

"I found it." At her slightly strangled tone, Jack looked up. "*Marine* is in the FBI stolen art database. The Monet—along with several other valuable paintings—was stolen from a museum in Rio de Janeiro during Carnival in 2006. Hasn't been seen since." Zoe shifted the laptop so Jack could see the landscape, a sweep of a deep blue bay rimmed with land in neutral tans, yellows, and greens that transitioned to a pale wedge of a low, white escarpment that stretched out into the water forming one arm of the bay.

Jack came closer to look at the image of the painting on the computer. "It makes sense."

"Of course. I should have seen that one coming." Zoe slid off the barstool and paced as she spoke. "He was a criminal. Of course he wouldn't do something as out of character as buy something legitimately for sale. No, it had to be black market art."

"Zoe," Jack leaned forward. "This is actually good."

"How? How can this be good?"

"If we find it, there are two parties interested in it—the FBI and Mr. Gray. Now, I may be way off base here, but I'm assuming that since Mr. Gray wants a stolen painting, he's probably involved in other illegal activities that would interest the FBI."

"You mean besides murder?"

"We know about Lucinda's murder and a stolen painting, but I'm willing to bet that those aren't his first forays into illegal activity."

Zoe walked slowly toward him. "You're saying that if we find the painting, we can use it."

"It's leverage."

"With the FBI and with Mr. Gray." They smiled at each other for a second across the island. Then Zoe said, "We need to know more about Mr. Gray." She'd climbed halfway onto the barstool before it hit her. She stopped, leg dangling. "Jack. The people. We're looking at this the wrong way. It's not the painting, it's the people we need to focus on."

"You're right," Jack agreed. "We need everything we can get on this Darius Gray."

Zoe shifted her weight fully into the barstool and began typing. "Let's see what Google has to say about him." She summarized as she scanned. "Okay, he's in the import/export business, but he was arrested over a year ago." She swiveled the laptop so Jack could see a news article with a photo that showed a nearly bald man with circular glasses and neatly trimmed gray beard, who wore a three-piece suit while being escorted out of an office building between two police officers.

"Not what I expected him to look like," Zoe said. The image she'd had in mind of him ran more along the lines of Marlon Brando in *The Godfather*. "This guy looks more like a college professor than a criminal. But, no matter what he looks like, he's apparently got some really good lawyers," Zoe continued. "He was charged with money laundering, tax evasion, and handling stolen goods. He was convicted on the tax evasion and money laundering charges and went to prison in January."

"So maybe not such great lawyers," Jack said.

Zoe held up a finger. "He got off on a technicality during the appeal." She clicked on another article, this one with a picture of Gray waving to the camera, a smile splitting his beard, as he stepped into a limousine. "He's been out of prison for two weeks, which explains why he's just now coming after the painting, I guess," Zoe said.

Jack nodded. "I suppose a federal trial and prison time would take priority over recovering a painting that you'd been swindled out of."

"But if he's fresh out of prison, why would he come after the painting?" Zoe asked. "Wouldn't it be smarter for him to wait? Wouldn't the FBI—or whoever investigated him before —have an eye on him?"

"You'd think they would, wouldn't you?"

"As close as they've watched me, trying to get to you, I can't believe they'd wouldn't do the same thing to him. This is the third time he's been arrested, the second time he's gone to jail, and the second time he's walked away."

"Maybe he feels invincible," Jack said. "Like he can get away with whatever he wants." He ran his hand through his hair. "It's not enough. We don't even know if the authorities are still interested in him."

"Wait—I know someone..." Zoe's voice trailed off as she typed.

"Who?"

"There. Message sent," Zoe said. "If there's anything else to find out about Mr. Darius Gray, Jenny will dig it up. She's got contacts in the FBI—she's a friend of Mort's. I can't believe I didn't think of her a minute ago."

"Who is this again?"

"Jenny Singletarry. You remember her, the reporter who broke the story about the fraud. I answered a few of her questions once the FBI cleared you."

"You talked to the media?" Jack's tone implied it was equivalent to spreading the plague. "And you emailed her now?"

"Yes. She was so persistent. I figured if I talked to her, gave her a little info, she'd move on. It worked. It was a fair article, and I haven't heard from her since. Well, except for *her* Facebook friend request, which I accepted."

Jack rubbed his forehead. "Well, we can't undo it now."

"She's good, Jack, and I trust her."

Jack waved his hand. "It's done. Can't change it. Got to move on. Maybe she'll find something useful, if she's got the resources you say she does. It's always good to know what kind of person we are dealing with."

Zoe sat up straight. "Jack, we do know the person we're dealing with," she said, excitement quickening the pace of her words. "Not just Gray. Anna. We know Anna has the painting. Mr. Gray doesn't know that. He thinks we've got it. We know who really has it."

Jack nodded. "Find Anna, and we find the painting—at least we hope. I see what you're saying, but I doubt she is broadcasting her presence."

"I agree. She probably isn't tweeting about her day, but I think I know someone who can help us find her."

"Who?"

"A reformed hacker."

SPECIAL Agent Greg Sato leaned back from his desk and stretched. He'd tweaked a muscle in his lower back, and it was tightening up like a rubber band snapping back into shape after it had been stretched to full length. He shouldn't have pushed so hard during his run last night, but the half marathon was two weeks away and he needed to get his miles in. As he stretched, he glanced at the wonder kid, who was hunched over a nearby desk. Supposedly a Golden Boy and a fast burner, Dirk Sorkensov was the youngest agent Sato had ever worked with. He was so shiny and fresh-faced that the corners of his eyes didn't even wrinkle when he smiled. And he smiled a lot. Good-humored to the point of irritation, Wonder Kid could always find the bright side to any situation.

Too many cases? Job security, he'd pronounce cheerfully.

Called in to work the weekend? Bonus! Overtime.

No witnesses? A challenge.

Sato was beginning to think Wonder Kid had been promoted because of his upbeat, always positive attitude.

Sato twisted slowly to the left, felt the tension release a bit, then turned to the right and watched Wonder Kid, whose attention was equally divided between a file on his desk and his cell phone, which he checked every few minutes.

Sato finished his stretch as The Kid closed the file with a whistle. "Man, this reads like a novel." He stood and came over to Sato's desk, bringing the file with him. "Fascinating."

Sato grunted. He hadn't thought he'd miss his old partner much, but this was one of those days when he wished he could exchange The Kid's puppyish enthusiasm for Mort's silent world-weariness. Must be his back making him cranky. Sato didn't need to see the name on the file. "The Andrews case? Yeah." The Kid shot a quick look at his phone as he handed Sato the file. "Anything?" Sato asked with a pointed glance at the phone.

"No. Just Braxton Hicks."

"Oh." Sato had no idea what Braxton Hicks were, but The Kid's wife—*wife*! He looked as if he was barely old enough to have a high school diploma—and she was pregnant. Sato figured Braxton Hicks had to be something to do with the pregnancy. Before The Kid could enlighten him, Sato said, "The one disappointment of that case was the low arrest rate. All the big fish got away."

"Dying isn't exactly getting away."

Sato shrugged. "No arrests."

"Well, here's a chance to change that." The Kid held out an additional stack of papers. "Got the report on the transfers of the money from the scam."

At least The Kid liked reading reports and getting into the hard evidence as much as Mort had, Sato thought. Sato preferred to focus on more intangible things: attitudes, relationships, and connections. "It's about time."

Sato took the papers and skimmed them as The Kid said, "The ex of Jack Andrews. Zoe Hunter."

Sato went back to the first page and read through them again. "Zoe Hunter managed to siphon off several million dollars from the scam and then got it into an off-shore account in a roundabout way that took us months to trace? Then she bought something from an art dealer?" He shifted in his chair and his back tweaked, but he barely noticed it. "Interesting. Let's go see her."

7

Jack parked in front of a modest one-story brown brick rancher. They climbed out and walked up the sidewalk between low boxwood hedges. "This is where your hacker lives?"

"Reformed hacker." Zoe handed Jack one of the bags of Chinese takeout as her phone chimed, signaling she had a new text. "That's weird. The message space is blank. There's only a photo attached." Zoe opened the link and frowned. "Why would Helen send me a picture of her house? I know what it looks like."

Jack shrugged. "Maybe she sent it to the wrong number."

"No, wait. It's not her number. I don't know who sent this." As she spoke another blank text with a picture attached popped up. The next photo was another of Helen, this time standing on her porch, signing for a UPS package. A third photo arrived, Helen walking into the building where she worked at the county offices. The next message didn't have a photo. It read, "Don't forget our agreement. We know where your friends live and work."

Zoe's stomach flipped. "Oscar. It's got to be him. That creep is following Helen around. He better not go near her. I have to call her—"

Jack caught her hand as they arrived on the porch. "The less she knows the better."

"I know that's how you were trained, but that doesn't always work out so good. Forewarned is forearmed."

"What are you going to tell her? That a man is watching her? That's not going to make her feel better. It will just scare her."

Zoe fingered the buttons on the phone. She didn't want to frighten Helen, and she couldn't order her to stay indoors without telling her everything that was going on.

"Oscar won't do anything." Jack's tone was steady. "He wants your cooperation. Those photos are a reminder, to keep you—us—focused."

"I can't let him hurt Helen."

"Hurting her gains him nothing. If anything, it would distract us from getting the painting. He doesn't want that. Every move he and Gray make is calculated. They're not psychopaths attacking women for the thrill of it. Gray wants his painting, and he thinks you can get it. If you get distracted worrying about Helen and get sucked into telling her everything that's going on, it will only slow us down."

Jack was right. Sometimes she hated it when he was right. So logical and reasoned. She wanted to do something. "Okay. No call—yet." Zoe punched the doorbell with more force than was necessary, wishing it was Oscar's nose.

"Keeping her out of the loop is the best thing you can do for her."

A slim woman in her twenties with an upturned nose, dark brown eyes, and pale blond hair caught up in a ponytail opened the door. She wore dark jeans, pointy-toed cowboy boots, and a loose, gauzy shirt that floated around her as she stepped back, waving them inside. "Zoe," she exclaimed, "You didn't have to bring dinner."

Zoe forced herself to switch her thoughts away from the photos to Carla. "It's the least we could do, barging in on you like this at the last minute."

"And you must be the elusive Jack. Come in. I'm Carla." As she closed the door, she stepped close to Zoe and murmured, "Nice," with raised eyebrows.

A girl about five years old in a pink leotard and tights whizzed by. "This is my niece, Emma," Carla said at normal volume. "Stop running for a minute and say hello to my friends, Emma."

Emma skidded to a stop on the tile floor, whispered *hello*, and scampered off again, flitting like a hummingbird collecting nectar.

"My sister had a meeting, so I took Emma to dance class tonight," Carla explained as she led the way through the open plan living room decorated in shades of gray, white, and navy blue to a kitchen painted a sunny yellow with white cabinets. She placed the food on a rectangular wooden dining table positioned along a row of tall windows that looked out onto her patio and fenced backyard.

"Her mom will be along soon, but we should go ahead and eat." She opened a cabinet and began removing glasses.

While her back was turned, Jack sent Zoe a doubtful look.

"What?" she mouthed at him, and he gave a pointed glance at Carla's back, then around the room.

"Are you sure about Carla?" he asked in an undertone.

Carla turned from the cabinet, carrying several glasses. She had one in her right hand and pointed it at Jack. "I know that look." She plunked the glasses down on the table and turned to Zoe. "I swear I should go back to the Goth look. No one takes me seriously. I think it's the hair." She swiped a hand down her blond ponytail. She switched her attention back to Jack. "You think I'm some suburbanite who spends half her days in yoga pants at the gym and the other half on Pinterest, right?"

"Ah—no. I, um..."

"You don't think I could hack into my own email account, much less a high-tech website with layers of security protocols. Am I right?"

Jack cleared his throat and put his hands out, palms up. "Sorry. I apologize. I made assumptions based on your surroundings. I have to admit that I didn't expect a hacker to have such a...homey place." He gestured at a potted orange Gerbera daisy in the center of the table.

"Don't worry. I won't hold it against you." She gave him a stack of napkins—white polka dots on yellow—and opened a drawer for silverware. "And technically, I'm an information technology and security consultant." She cocked her head to one side. "Do you think if I lived in a grungy, dark studio apartment strewn with empty pizza boxes, I'd have more clients?"

Zoe looked around. "Definitely."

Carla crunched up her shoulders. "I could never do it. I love this house."

"You could always rent office space. You could use it only to meet clients. Make it nice and dreary. Paint the walls a dark gray, keep the blinds closed, and scatter around lots of computer equipment and extension cords. I bet your client list would double. I'd let you try it for free for a few weeks next time someone moves out of one of my office suites."

"Maybe."

Emma climbed into a chair, and they sat down to eat. By the time they had the boxes open, Emma was deep into an interrogation of Jack. "What's your favorite color?"

Jack paused with his chopsticks poised over his fried rice. "I'd have to say blue."

"Like your eyes," Emma said. "Mine is purple."

"Not pink?" Jack asked.

"No. Pink is for babies. I *have* to wear it for ballet."

"I see."

Carla cleared her throat. "Don't forget to eat your shrimp, Emma."

Jack turned to Carla. "So Goth?"

Zoe looked pointedly at the daffodil yellow kitchen. "It is hard to believe, isn't it?"

"I *was*. Get Zoe to show you my picture junior year. I look like something out of a bad horror movie. Jet-black hair, thick eyeliner, and I already had the pallor because I was so fair-skinned. I hung out with the stoners behind the Quick-Mart." She looped a noodle around her chopsticks. "Senior year I took a programming class and that was it for the Goth thing. I'd found myself. Turns out I'm a geek."

Emma said, "I have a turtle."

"What's your turtle's name?" Zoe asked.

"Speedy. Daddy says it's moronic."

"I think you mean *ironic*, sweetie," Carla corrected, hiding a smile behind her glass.

Emma shrugged. She focused her attention on Jack. "We did have a parrot, but we had to find him a new home because he said bad words."

"I wonder where the parrot learned those words?" Zoe said, widening her eyes as she looked at Carla.

"It's a mystery." Carla stood and began closing the food containers.

"We don't say bad words," Emma informed them in a grave tone.

"That's right. We don't say bad words." In an undertone, Carla added, "Not anymore."

Zoe watched Emma out of the corner of her eye, struggling to break open a plastic fortune cookie wrapper. Jack offered to help. Emma put it in his hand, and he ripped it open. Zoe grabbed the empty container of fried rice and followed Carla into the kitchen.

"That stuff I told you about on the phone, the favor I need, forget it."

Carla closed the refrigerator door and turned to her. "What are you talking about? Of course I'll help you."

"I know, but I don't want to put you in a bad position." Zoe looked to the table where Jack was reading Emma's fortune to her. "I can't ask you to take a risk for me. You're not a hacker anymore. I can't ask you to break the law for me."

"It's true that I've come back from—the dark side, let's say—but I didn't do it because I was afraid I'd get caught. I decided I wanted to do something more significant with my life than try to create a virus that made millions of people curse at their monitors."

"There you go. I can't ask you to bend your standards. It's been great seeing you. We'll get out of your hair. Forget I ever asked."

Carla dumped the leftover sauce packets into the trash and let the lid clang shut. "I stopped hacking because I decided to use my powers for good, not evil, as the cliché goes. It sounds like you could use my help. You said you can't go to the police, right?"

"No, not now." Zoe hadn't told her the details of what had happened, only that she was in trouble and needed information that she couldn't find herself.

"Okay, then. Let me work my magic and worry about my conscience. Sometimes you have to bend the rules a bit to get at the truth. That's the old hacker in me talking, but there is some truth there. Come on, you like to live on the edge, don't you understand?"

"Of course, I understand taking risks. That's practically my motto, but I don't want to put anyone else at risk."

"Zoe, I'm not going to get caught. What you need is easy-peasy. Child's play. I'm not going to take any chances that would put me in a bad position. But I'm not going to stand by and let things get worse for you either, not when I can take a teeny, tiny peek and—possibly—give you some answers."

"I don't know..." Emma had left the table, and Jack was gathering up the last of the food boxes and chopsticks while Emma jumped on the couch like it was a diving board.

Carla crossed her arms. "Zoe, you already told me what you need to know."

Zoe sighed. "And you're curious now, so you're going to look it up anyway whether or not I try and talk you out of it."

"Yep. That's about the size of it."

Zoe thought of the photos of Helen going about her day, completely unaware that Oscar was shadowing her. "Okay, you win. You can hack for me."

EMMA'S mom arrived shortly after dinner. After waving good-bye to them, Carla motioned for Zoe and Jack to follow her into a spare bedroom she'd made into an office. She bypassed the large glass desk with its sleek computer and opened the folding closet doors, revealing a second work area with several monitors, CPUs, and a tangle of cords. "My special work space," she explained.

Zoe took a seat in the rolling office chair at the glass desk and Jack leaned against the room's doorframe with his arms crossed. Carla swiveled her chair side-to-side, fingers poised on the keyboard. "Let's see what we can do. Okay, so we've got the name Anna Whitmore and a physical description. No phone number, address, friends, family, or business ties."

A gloomy sense of the impossibility of the task she'd asked Carla to accomplish settled on Zoe. "It's a pathetically small amount of info, I know." It was worse than looking for a needle in a haystack. This was like looking for a needle in Montana.

"She said something once that made me think she was from the Pacific Northwest. What was it?" Jack frowned at the floor. "It was snowing—really coming down." His head popped up. "She said at least it wasn't rain. After four years in Seattle, she'd take snow over rain any day."

"That's good," Carla said, and then went quiet as she typed away for a bit. Eventually, she pushed back so they could both see the monitor. "Any of these people look like her?"

Zoe and Jack both moved closer to the monitor. "Facebook?" Zoe asked, skimming the list of faces.

"Yep. It's a good place to start. So many people have profiles—even if they're not active on the site. It's a gold mine of information," Carla said. "The name Anna Whitmore isn't that common, and I narrowed the results by region. Nothing here? Okay, next page."

Zoe shook her head as Carla scrolled through two more pages.

"Wait." Zoe pointed at a photo of an attractive woman with dark hair. "I think that's her. Her hair is longer than when I saw her, but the face is the same."

"Looks like her profile is private. Let me see what I can do." Carla hummed a few bars of *Smoke on the Water* as she typed. Zoe eased back a few steps so she wouldn't be looming over Carla, but she was completely focused on the computer, her fingers tapping away at the keys. Jack sent Zoe a raised eyebrow look. Zoe shrugged.

After a few minutes, Carla leaned back. "We're in." Zoe and Jack closed the distance and looked over Carla's shoulder as she read, "Hometown, Chicago. College at the University of Washington," she said with a nod at Jack. "Her last employer is listed as ComTech in San Bernardino, California."

"Must have wanted some sun after all that rain," Zoe said. "What else?"

"Nothing recent. She hasn't posted a status update since she went on a vacation almost three years ago. The last updates are photos of her on a beach in Saint-Tropez." Carla switched to the contact information page. "Excellent." A smile spread across her face. "Email addresses, just what we need. The Facebook.com address probably doesn't have much," she said, her fingers already tapping the keyboard. "I don't know anyone who actually uses their Facebook email address. I'll concentrate on the Yahoo address." She typed a few strokes, paused, then said under her breath, "Okay, let's try it another way."

Finally, she hit ENTER like a concert pianist striking the final key during a performance of Beethoven's Fifth and spun toward them, eyes shining. "What did I tell you? Easy-peasy. You're in luck. Looks like she still uses this email account."

"What are her most recent emails?" Jack asked.

"Um...well, I think we can assume she's a shopper. Maybe a shopaholic. She's got emails in here from Nordstrom, Neiman Marcus, Gucci, Versace, Dolce & Gabbana, and Armani as well as a couple of other ones that I haven't heard of, but I bet they're expensive." Her voice changed. "Now this is interesting. Some airline ticket confirmations. Four days ago she was scheduled to fly from Naples, Italy to Paris."

Zoe and Jack exchanged a glance. "It fits with what Oscar told us," Jack said.

"But Naples?" Zoe said, "Do you think she's there?"

"No idea," Jack said, "but it's a start."

"Naples," Zoe muttered. "It always seems to come back to Naples." She and Jack had traveled to Naples last year in an attempt to discover who was behind the fraud at Jack's company.

She thumped down in the other office chair. "It's a start, but Naples is huge. Can you narrow down where she's sending the emails from? Can you get a location on her computer...or something?"

Carla shook her head. "Nope, I already checked. She's a little lax on password security—that's how I got into her account, but she does use a virtual private network to hide her IP address. I traced it back through a couple of European servers to a location in Nevada, but couldn't get farther than that. I can work on it though."

"Don't sound so eager," Zoe said. "I think you'd better step away from the computer. I feel a bit like I've bought a drink for an alcoholic who's been on the wagon."

"It was fun. I haven't done anything like that in years. But you're right, I don't want to go back there," she said with a sigh. "Not if I want to keep my day job, anyway. There's a second airline reservation. She's flying into Paris again. Departs Naples on the fifteenth and returns on the sixteenth."

"The fifteenth? That's tomorrow." Zoe and Jack exchanged a look. Zoe hopped up and crossed the room so she could study the computer herself. "She arrives at six. She could be going back to the gallery. Do you think we can do it?"

Carla looked back and forth between them. "Do what?"

"It's probably our best chance," Jack said. "If we can make a flight tonight we could arrive about the same time as her."

"But the tickets. They'd be outrageous."

"We'll charge them."

"But they have to be paid off sometime," Zoe said.

"I'll cover it. You'd do the same thing for me. In fact, you *have* done the same thing for me."

Carla had been watching their conversation like a spectator at a tennis match, her gaze bobbing back and forth between them. "Y'all aren't talking about flying to Paris, are you? Tonight? That's crazy."

Jack said, "Come on, Zoe. I have some money in savings and a credit card that hasn't been used in months. I couldn't touch it or the money while I was under the radar, but there's nothing stopping me from using it now. How much can two last minute tickets to Paris cost?"

"A couple of thousand, at least."

"I'll cover it. You can pay me back, if it makes you feel better."

"Okay," Zoe said reluctantly.

"You can't fly to Paris tonight," Carla said.

"Why not? We both have passports," Zoe said. "Dallas is an international hub. There will be plenty of flights. And for once, the FBI couldn't care less if I left the country."

"Not yet anyway," Jack said. "And we want to keep it that way. How much are the tickets, Carla? Can you look it up for us?"

"And could you print her most recent emails for us?" Zoe added. "I can look through them on the flight, see if I can find anything else."

Carla turned back to the computer. "You're both crazy. You don't just book an international trip and hop on a plane a couple of hours later. You need time. You have to buy guidebooks, plan your itinerary. You don't even know what electrical adaptors you need."

"Don't worry. I'm getting used to it," Zoe said.

SATO pressed the doorbell again. The Kid waited behind his shoulder, glancing at his phone. It was late, and Sato knew The Kid wanted to get home. An issue with another case had consumed the rest of the afternoon and early evening. They hadn't been able to get out of the office until after six-thirty. Sato had told The Kid to go on...that he could handle the check in with Zoe Hunter on his own, but The Kid had said he wanted to meet the "cyber thief."

After a few minutes, Sato went around back, pounded on the kitchen door. No answer. He hadn't called, not wanting to give Zoe Hunter or the newly cleared Mr. Andrews any warning he was coming. He cupped his hand around his eyes and looked in the window over the sink.

A wadded dishtowel sat on the counter. Two tall glasses

along with a few pieces of silverware rested in the sink. A smattering of paper, which looked like envelopes, trailed across the island as if someone had tossed them down on the way in from the mailbox. "Apparently, they are both out." He stepped away, then went back and peered at the kitchen ceiling. Yep, the gaping hole in the drywall was finally fixed. Unfortunately, he didn't think he could take that as confirmation that Zoe had taken millions of dollars from a scam and hid it in a well-disguised bank account.

Sato turned from the window and surveyed the backyard where The Kid was pacing, checking the signal on his phone. "Looks like they've done some landscaping, too," Sato commented.

"So you think she took the money?" The Kid asked with a nod of his head toward the house and a doubtful look.

"The house and neighborhood don't exactly scream millionaire, do they?"

"No, but I suppose she could just be smart. You know, waiting it out so she doesn't raise any suspicions."

"Except for purchasing art," Sato said.

"You've been in there before," The Kid said pointing to the house. "Is she into art?"

"Only art I saw in there was mass market stuff, posters you can get at Target or IKEA. And unless she put up a very good front, she's not any more computer savvy than your average Joe."

The Kid's phone beeped. He studied the screen. "This is it?" he read in a puzzled voice. He looked at Sato. "What does that mean, *this is it?*

"Who's it from?" Sato asked.

"Sophie. Do you think…? She's not…?"

"You better go find out."

The Kid shot him a look of excitement mixed with terror before he shot off around the corner of the house. For a nanosecond, Sato felt a nudge of something almost like longing. He'd never run like that in his life, not even in the last half marathon.

He gave himself a mental shake. What was he, crazy? He didn't want to be that tied to another individual, to have his hopes and dreams, his whole life, wrapped up in someone else.

The Kid reappeared. "You have the keys," he called as he sprinted toward Sato.

"I knew there was a reason you got promoted so fast. You're sharp. Took you less than a minute to figure that out." Sato tossed the keys to The Kid.

The Kid made a strangled sound. "Come on, we've got to go."

"You take the car. I'll call a friend to pick me up." The Kid was gone before Sato finished his sentence.

He walked across the backyard and paused with his hands in his pockets to study the row of hedges against the back fence. Not extravagant, by any means. Extravagant would be a pool or an outdoor kitchen.

He turned away, making a mental note to drop by again tomorrow, then he pulled out his phone and scrolled through the contact list. Ah, yes, Deborah lived a few blocks away. Maybe she was home...

8

Zoe glanced at her watch as they hurried through Charles de Gaulle Airport. "We're too late." Their connecting flight through London had a weather delay, putting them an hour behind their scheduled arrival time. "Her flight probably just landed." Because their flight was international, they'd arrived into Charles de Gaulle, while Anna's regional flight from Naples was arriving at Paris's other major airport, Orly. "Do you think Anna's flight could be delayed, too?"

"It's possible, but I don't think we should count on it," Jack said, steering their single rolling suitcase through the airport. "I think we better go directly to Gallery Twenty-Seven and hope we can catch her there. Taxi or train?" Jack asked.

Zoe had spent some of the flight skimming the Paris *Smart Travel* guidebook she'd bought in the DFW airport. She hadn't copy-edited a Paris or France guidebook, but felt she could find any info they needed. "Train, I think. It's late in the day and traffic might be bad."

Jack nodded and they followed the signs to the train,

bought their tickets, and squeezed into one of the cars going into the city. "So the hotel is close to the gallery?" Zoe asked as she turned to the Metro map.

"Yes. Right across the street. It's in the Seventh Arrondissement, near the Eiffel Tower." While Zoe had been buying the guidebook, Jack had used the time at the airport gate to find and book them a hotel, saying he better make the most of the free Wi-Fi in the airport.

"Okay, Eiffel Tower it is," Zoe said with a little shiver of excitement. The Eiffel Tower. This wasn't exactly the way she'd dreamed of touring the City of Light, but she was here, and she was certainly going to take in all of Paris that she could—even a glimpse of Paris was better than no Paris at all. Of course she couldn't see anything picture-postcard right now—they were whizzing through the suburbs—but they would be in the center of the city soon. "We caught the express, did you notice that?" Zoe said. "That's good."

They were wedged into the center of the train compartment, and Jack looked over his shoulder at her as he asked, "Good, because we'll get to the gallery faster? Or, good, because we'll get into Paris faster?"

Zoe closed the guidebook. "To the gallery, of course."

Jack lowered his chin. "I know you better than that. I bet you've already mapped out at least three major tourist sites we'll see on the way to the gallery."

"Only two," Zoe admitted. "If we get off at the Alma Marceau stop, we'll be able to see the Eiffel Tower and cross the Pont de l'Alma bridge over the Seine."

"That's my girl."

Zoe tried to tell herself she didn't feel a warm glow at those words. "It's only a few blocks from the gallery. Really."

"Fine by me. Might as well see what we can while we're here."

"My thoughts exactly."

After changing to another line, they emerged from the Metro and didn't have to look hard to find the tallest structure in Paris. The graceful lines of the tower stood out sharply against the tangerine sky of sunset. Zoe came to a stop. "Wow. Can you believe people hated it when it first went up?"

"Really? Let's move over here out of the way." Jack took her elbow, and they shifted to the side, out of the middle of the busy sidewalk.

"Yep. They thought it was ugly, a monstrosity." Zoe snapped a few pictures with her phone.

"You better let me navigate." Jack took the guidebook from her hand. "You're in full-on tourist daze."

"Yes, I am," Zoe said happily. "It was built for a World Exhibition, and some people wanted it torn down immediately. Can you imagine?" Zoe put her phone away, leaned over Jack's shoulder to see the map. "We take a left. The gallery is a couple of blocks away." She hooked her arm through his elbow and pointed at the gold dome on the skyline. "We head that way, toward Napoleon's tomb. Slightly strange that he's buried here, isn't it?" Zoe said.

"Considering that they exiled him? I'll say. Although, he is one of the most famous Frenchmen in history." As they strolled along streets with five- and six-story buildings with cream-colored stone facades that contrasted with the distinctively French-style sloping dark mansard roofs, Jack commented, "Swanky." At street level, they passed shop windows displaying spring fashions, small hotels with shiny name plaques, and cafés with awnings stretching over tables on the sidewalk. Above, through the tracery of tree branches scattered with buds of green, dark shutters bracketed iron balconies.

"Speaking of swanky." Zoe tilted her head, "There's Gallery Twenty-Seven." They came even with a shop with an arched doorway. The window display was an Impressionist seascape, an intricately patterned Turkish rug, and a pair of silver candlesticks.

"Then this is our hotel." Jack crossed to a pair of wooden doors inset with glass on the other side of the street. The doors swished open as they approached.

The desk clerk at the Hotel Madeleine welcomed them, took down their passport information, swiped Jack's credit card, and then directed them up two flights of curving stairs, pointing out the minuscule elevator. Zoe thought their suitcase might possibly fit inside, but there was no way a person *and* a suitcase would fit inside.

Jack swung open the door of Room Seven and went straight to the window while Zoe looked around. The walls were white and covered with loads of molding and trim. A small crystal chandelier glittered overhead. Jack pulled back the sheer curtains, revealing two floor-to-ceiling windows.

"Excellent," he said. "We can see the gallery, and it looks like there are living quarters directly above it." He squinted. "Yes, there's a spiral staircase on the second floor that must go down to the shop. I bet the owner lives above."

Zoe wasn't worried about the view. "Ah—Jack, the room is kind of small." The room itself was narrow, only a few feet wider than the bed, which was a confection of pale pink pillows and ruffles. It was designed for one person, and a small one, at that. Someone who could fit into that elevator.

"Because it's a single room." Jack walked toward her.

"Oh, don't tell me it was the last room they had, and we have to share. That's just too, too—"

"Trite? I agree." He stopped a few inches from her and reached for her hand. "That's why I'm next door." He put the old fashioned, oversized bronze key in her palm and curled her fingers over it.

Zoe cleared her throat. "Right." She inched backward because the small room now seemed even more minuscule with Jack so close to her. Her calves bumped into the bed.

"I'm courting you, remember? Taking things slowly."

"Wooing. Right."

He leaned forward and brushed a kiss along her cheekbone, and all sorts of tingly sensations fired through her. "Get some rest, if you want. I'll be next door, watching the gallery." He left through an adjoining door, pulling it closed behind him. Zoe collapsed onto the narrow bed, her heart skittering. There was something to be said for this going slow. It was kind of delicious.

THE sound of a door closing woke Zoe out of a deep sleep. It took a second for the narrow bed, white woodwork, and gauzy curtains framing the windows to make sense. Paris. She was in Paris. It was dark now, and windows glowed in the building directly across from the hotel. She rubbed her hand across her forehead, remembering that very chaste kiss on the cheek Jack had given her before she left and the warm, fuzzy glow it had set off inside her.

She sat up abruptly. Jet lag. That had to be why she'd gone all mushy. She unzipped the suitcase with a vicious tug. She'd thought Jack's attentions might taper off, but it was clear she'd have to do something. She couldn't let it go on. It wasn't fair to Jack. There was no way she wanted to replay the disaster of their divorce. And dating Jack again or...anything else...would have the same outcome. It would, no matter what Jack or Helen thought.

Out of the corner of her eye, a flash of light caught her attention. She could see just the top of the Eiffel Tower, glowing golden in the dark. Twin beacons of light at the top of the tower swept across the black sky. She sighed. Okay, so maybe she wouldn't say anything just yet. They were in Paris, after all.

She took a quick shower in the tiny en suite bathroom wedged into the corner of her room, then eyed the clothes she'd hurriedly tossed in the suitcase. Her packing had been slightly haphazard because her laundry hamper at home was overflowing, so her choices had been limited. She hadn't had time to check the weather so she'd tried to cover all the bases. She'd thrown in a couple of long-sleeved shirts, jeans, a few tanks for layering, a simple wrap dress that didn't wrinkle, a sweater, and a pair of capris, along with some sandals. She picked a long-sleeved pink shirt and jeans. She eased her shirt over her head, careful to avoid the tender lump at the base of her skull. It was still sore, but the swelling had gone down. She gingerly combed her hair then slipped on a navy sweater because the temperature had dropped with the sunset.

She tapped on the adjoining door, and Jack called out for her to come in.

His room was identical to hers. The lights were off, and he stood at the windows, a pair of binoculars at his face. He was wearing fresh clothes as well—a lightweight gray sweater with the sleeves pushed up. "Feel better?"

"Yes. Did you get some sleep?"

"Nah, I got enough on the plane."

"That's an understatement," Zoe said. Unlike Zoe, who was an insomniac on an airplane, Jack could sleep soundly from takeoff to landing.

"It's a gift," Jack said. "I picked up some sandwiches from the café around the corner if you're hungry." Crinkled white paper covered the mirrored desktop.

Zoe took a sandwich with thin slices of ham, cheese, and buttered bread then joined Jack at the window. "You pack binoculars when you travel?"

"Always."

"Hmm. I'll have to put that on my essentials list." She finished off the sandwich and reached for a small cup of chocolate and a plastic spoon. "What's this? Pudding?"

"The woman at the café said it's a custard. *Petit-pots*, she called them."

"It's delicious," Zoe said after a bite of the creamy chocolate. She pointed at the window with her spoon. "Anything?"

"Not really. I've seen a man—kind of heavy with slicked back hair—Masard, the owner. I found an article on-line about the gallery with his picture. There's a younger blond woman—his assistant, I think—who has been moving around, closing up. The woman just left, and Masard locked up." Jack handed over the binoculars and went to the bed where her laptop was open. "I hope you don't mind."

"No, of course not. *Mi* laptop is *su* laptop."

"I used the log-in and password that Carla gave us to check Anna's email, but nothing new."

Zoe put the binoculars to her face and adjusted them. The gallery windows jumped into focus. She shifted her gaze higher and saw the heavy-set man moving around the second floor, which had a kitchenette with a sink and hotplate on the countertop along one wall. The rest of the room was set up like an office with heavy furniture, file cabinets, and a couple of armchairs positioned in front of a fireplace. "He's making a cup of tea, it looks like."

"Yeah, exciting stuff. I watched him file papers."

"So what do we do if we've completely missed Anna?" Zoe asked, voicing her worst fear.

"I don't know. It was a gamble, coming here. I guess we keep monitoring her email, see if she gives something else away."

Zoe left the windows and swiveled the laptop toward her, hitting the refresh button. "I wish we at least knew where she was staying."

"She probably didn't have her hotel reservation sent to her email. Or, she used another email address."

"We don't even know for sure that she's in Paris. This whole thing could be an enormous waste of time." Zoe thought of those photos of Helen. What if they were on the wrong track? If something didn't turn up soon, she'd have to call Helen and warn her, no matter how restrained Jack thought Oscar would be.

"Not a complete waste. You've checked the Eiffel Tower off your bucket list."

Zoe sent him a crooked smile. "True, but that won't be much of a comfort when I'm in prison." Or if Helen gets hurt, she silently added, but kept that thought to herself, not wanting to rehash the argument with Jack.

Jack reached for a sandwich. "Let's not start measuring you for an orange jumpsuit just yet. I do think Anna is here. If she'd changed or cancelled her reservation, there would most likely be an email since she had her flight details sent to her via email."

"Okay, I agree with you there. But it doesn't do us much good if we can't find her." Zoe hit refresh on the web page and tensed. "Oh, it's just junk mail," she said, her shoulders sagging. "Twenty percent off shipping at Macy's this weekend."

They ate their sandwiches and watched Masard eat a dinner of crusty bread and soup while he did paperwork. Zoe brushed the crumbs from her fingers and opened a bottle of fizzy water, then paced around the room, her mind skipping from one problem to the next. Every step in their precarious Rube Goldberg-like plan was riddled with potential problems. They weren't even sure Anna was in Paris, or if she had the painting, or how they'd get it from her.

If all that happened to work out, then there was a whole new set of problems, including how to use the painting. She agreed with Jack that it was leverage, but for it to help them, they needed the right people on their side, and how were they going to accomplish that? She supposed she could call Agent Sato. She demoted that idea to the "last resort" category as she crossed the room. The idea of going to a U.S. Embassy or Consulate flitted through her mind, but she thought that route would be fraught with red tape.

Jack didn't move the binoculars from his face as he spoke. "What's wrong?"

"Hmm? Oh, nothing," Zoe murmured, deep in thought. There was really only one person she trusted to help them out of this situation.

Jack removed the binoculars and looked at her. "You only pace like that when you're upset. Come on, tell me what's wrong."

Zoe twisted the bottle cap open and closed as she walked. “You know long-range planning isn’t my thing, but I can’t help thinking about what we’ll do, if we get the painting. If we’re going to use it to our advantage, not just hand it over to Mr. Gray, we’ve got to contact someone in...law enforcement. I think we’d better figure out who that is and how we’re going to do it.”

Jack ran his hand through his hair. “The logical place to go is the FBI’s art crime unit.”

“The one with the website that lists *Marine* as missing.” Zoe went to the laptop and brought up the website. “Well, they have a legal attaché at the embassy here in Paris. Or, we can call or email the main office in Washington D.C.”

“Neither way seems ideal.”

“I know. It could take weeks for us to get through to the right people. What about you? Surely there’s someone you can call from your time at the consulate?” Zoe asked.

“That’s been years. I didn’t stay in touch with anyone, well, except a few and they’re not exactly in good standing now.”

“There’s no one else?”

“No, we may have to call Sato.”

“I’d feel better if we had a few other options.” Zoe stood and walked again. She’d made two circuits of the room when she stopped. “Kathy,” she said and hurried to the computer.

“What?”

Zoe spoke as she typed. “Kathy. Why didn’t I think of this before? I should have checked this back in Dallas.”

“I’m lost.”

“The house sitter said Mort and Kathy were on a cruise. Kathy Vazarri,” she murmured as she scrolled down a webpage. "I was on Facebook a few weeks ago and got a friend suggestion."

"Still lost."

"Oh, that's right. You're Mr. Avoid Social Media."

"No, I just know better than to broadcast the details of my life."

"Anyway, Facebook sends messages every once in a while, saying, 'hey we see you know so-and-so, do you also know their friend, so-and-so?' I got one that had the name Kathy Vazarri on it. I remember it because it's an unusual name, but I didn't make the connection with Mort because it had a different name listed with it as well. Oh, I hope I didn't delete it. Wait, here it is. Kathy Bennett Vazarri. She's a friend of Jenny Singletarry, and Facebook wanted to know if I knew Kathy."

"Back to the reporter," Jack said with obvious distaste in his tone. "Any word from her?"

"No, nothing, which is kind of strange. Maybe she's out of town, too." Zoe looked through a list of names. "Yes! Here is his wife's profile. It's not even set on private. I can see all her updates." Her tone changed. "Oh. Nothing for the last three weeks, and it doesn't look like Mort has a Facebook account."

"Smart man."

"You don't get it, I know. But if this gets us in touch with Mort, you'll thank me later." Zoe straightened and began typing. She sent a friend request to Kathy along with a message, asking her to have Mort contact her with the note, "Please let him know it is urgent I talk to him."

She hit the send key and minimized the window. The webpage with Anna's email was still open, so Zoe hit the button to refresh the page. "Jack, there's a new email."

"Another twenty percent off sale?"

"No, the subject line is blank." She gulped water while she waited for the page with the message to load, then read it aloud. "Meet me at the pyramid behind the pyramid in forty-five minutes."

"That's it?" Jack asked, coming around to look over her shoulder.

"No signature, nothing. The sender's name is afriend@mymail.com. It's so vague; surely it's about the painting."

Jack nodded. "But a pyramid? In Paris. There's one at the Louvre."

"No, there's actually four," Zoe said, reaching for her guidebook. "There's one large one, the entrance to the museum, but there's three smaller ones positioned around it. There's also a stone pyramid somewhere else. I saw it in the guidebook. It looks like there's only one pyramid there, sort of a garden folly." She flipped a few pages. "There's also the Place des Pyramides, but it's not a pyramid. It's the name of a statue of Joan of Arc near the Louvre. The folly is farthest away in the north part of the city."

Jack glanced at his watch. "We don't have time to hit all three places."

"The Louvre seems most likely."

"Let's go."

9

Zoe reluctantly turned her back on the Arc de Triomphe du Carousel, which was quite a sight. One of Paris' "smaller" arches, it was dramatically topped with four horses pulling a chariot flanked with gold statues. They moved around a traffic circle to the Louvre.

Positioned in the center of the vast courtyard of the U-shaped palace that housed the Louvre, the large central glass pyramid that served as the main entry to the museum glowed in the darkness, its steep, sleek lines contrasting with the ornate curves of the one-time palace that surrounded it. Three smaller pyramids were set around the larger pyramid, one on the right, another on the left, and a third directly behind it. The museum was open late and, while the courtyard wasn't packed with people, there were more than a handful.

As they approached the large pyramid, Zoe said, "Technically, any one of the smaller pyramids could be 'behind' the larger pyramid. It depends on where you're standing."

"Yes," Jack agreed. "But my money is on the one in the

back. It's in alignment with the Arc and the larger pyramid."

"Good theory. I hope you're right," Zoe said as they hurried along the diagonal path between a fountain and the larger glass pyramid to the smaller one in the back. "I don't see her."

"We're early." Jack slipped his arm around Zoe's waist. "Let's stroll." The air had a sharp cold edge; spring hadn't fully arrived, but the sky was clear, and stars glowed along with the lights of the city. They circled the small pyramid then ambled around the courtyard. The leisurely pace set Zoe's teeth on edge. She wanted to move, make something happen, but there was nothing they could do, except wait. After another loop around the courtyard, Jack said, "I see her."

Zoe scanned the courtyard from the pyramids to the fountains to the museum and didn't see Anna. "Where?"

Jack stood behind Zoe, his hands on her shoulders, aiming her toward one of the fountains near the small pyramid. "There's your doppelganger, sitting on the ledge of the fountain. Third person from the left."

"That's not Anna..." Zoe protested, but her words died away as she recognized Anna's face under a mass of curly red hair. "She's in disguise," Zoe said, wonderingly. She'd heard what Oscar had said about the woman who wanted to sell the painting having red hair, but until this moment, Zoe had found it hard to believe that Anna would actually impersonate her. "Well, as weird as it is to see her being me, at least we found her."

Anna perched on the edge of the fountain, one slender leg crossed over the other, showing off a shapely calf and Louboutin pumps. She wore a camel-colored wool knee-length coat and a Burberry scarf. A heavy black bag weighed down her elbow, and a Marc Jacobs shopping bag sat at her feet.

"That wig is all wrong," Zoe said. It was too short; the fire engine red curls ended at Anna's chin, while Zoe's red hair with gold and bronze highlights fell to her shoulder blades.

Jack wrapped both arms around her waist and whispered in her ear, "Relax. We want to blend in with the crowd. We're just tourists taking in nighttime Paris."

"I'm blending."

"Not with that stare, you're not. You look like a hawk that has spotted a mouse. A very fat mouse."

"No way is Anna anywhere near fat. Perhaps I'm a tourist who finds the fountains and pyramids especially fascinating. Wait. Look at that guy who sat down beside Anna. Isn't that...?"

"Masard? Yes, it is."

Anna became very interested in her phone. Masard rearranged his scarf, tucking it more securely into the lapels of his coat then he checked his watch. Anna stood and walked away quickly, and Jack made a move to follow her, but Zoe gripped his arms. "Wait. The shopping bag. She left it."

After a few seconds, Masard picked up the bag and walked in the opposite direction from Anna.

They both hesitated then Zoe said, "We've got to follow the bag. It's big enough to have the painting in it."

"Yes, but we need to know where she's going, too. I'll take her; you follow him. Meet you back at the hotel."

"Right." Zoe said, but Jack was already walking away. Anna had left first. He had more ground to cover. Zoe's gaze flitted back and forth between Jack, who was shifting through the flow of people, and the black and white designer shopping bag Masard carried. When he rounded the corner of the fountain, moving between it and one of the other small pyramids, Zoe moved.

It was easy to keep track of the distinctive bag with large white letters spelling out the designer's name repeatedly over a black background. Zoe moved through the crowd, always staying a few people behind Masard, hoping he didn't hail a taxi. She had no idea how to say, "Follow that taxi," in French.

Fortunately, Masard skirted the traffic circle, strode through an archway, leaving the courtyard of the Louvre, then trotted down the steps under the curving art nouveau tulip lights at the Palais Royal and Musée du Louvre Metro entrance. Thank goodness, she and Jack had brought a *carnet*, a packet of ten tickets earlier, and split them. She only had to scramble through her messenger bag to find one and then slink into the same Metro car with Masard. She was afraid she'd lose sight of him if she rode in another car.

He didn't even look her way. He changed trains at Concorde, and Zoe had to run to keep up with him through the maze of white-tiled underground tunnels, but she managed to slip into the same car on the lilac colored Number Eight train, seconds before the doors closed.

As the train pulled away, Masard placed the shopping bag between his feet, crossed his hands over his paunch, and closed his eyes. When the train slowed for the École Militaire stop, his eyes popped open, and he moved to the door. There were a few other people exiting at the same stop, and Zoe let them leave first. She jogged across the platform, up the stairs, emerged to street level, and caught sight of him as he turned a corner.

This was a different Metro stop than the one she and Jack had used earlier, and the tangle of streets, tall buildings, and scattering of sidewalk cafés blocked any familiar landmarks that would have helped her get her bearings. She couldn't even see the Eiffel Tower. As she paced along behind Masard, she finally saw a familiar street name, one she'd seen earlier today. He was going back to the gallery.

Zoe kept back about half a block then hung back even more when he turned into the smaller street where the hotel and gallery were located. She turned the corner and collided with a blond-haired woman who stepped out of a doorway directly into her path. With a huff, the woman twitched her bright scarf back into place and moved on. Down the street, the gallery door closed.

After retrieving her key at the hotel front desk, Zoe skipped the tiny elevator, and took the curving stairs two at a time. Not bothering to turn on any lights, she went directly to the windows in her room. Masard was in the room above the gallery. "No, no, no," she muttered under her breath as Masard closed each set of interior shutters over the windows. The last thing Zoe saw was the black and white shopping bag on the worktable as he swung the final shutter into place.

She needed to see what was in that bag. Zoe hurried through the adjoining door to Jack's room, which they'd left open, and snatched up the binoculars from where he'd left them on the ledge near the window. Maybe she'd be able to see something through a sliver in the shutters.

The view was better out of her room, so she dashed back there in time to see one of the shutters swing inward a few inches, revealing a strip of the room, including part of the table. He hadn't latched the shutters, she realized as she put the binoculars to her eyes, edging to one side to maximize the tiny shard of the room that she could see. She could only see about half of the bag and Masard's hand as he reached into it.

He removed a bundle of fabric. Possibly a shawl because

there was a lot of fringe. He tossed it casually aside. He turned the bag on its side and worked a fold on the bottom open, then ran his hand along the long seam on the side, opening it. He splayed it flat, exposing the white lining.

He leaned close to the paper, bringing his face into Zoe's view. He adjusted his glasses as he teased one of the edges of the lining until he'd worked a finger between two layers of paper. Gently, he pulled the top layer of paper way, and Zoe caught her breath. Slowly, as if he were pulling a protective layer of plastic off a piece of electronics, Masard inched the white paper away, revealing the curve of land in tan, yellow, and green that contrasted with the deep blue of the water.

"That's it," Zoe whispered. The painting had been taken off the wooden frame that had once held it taut. She could still see the ridges where the frame had once run along the edge of the painted canvas.

Her phone rang, cutting loudly through the quiet of the room. She jerked, bobbling the binoculars. She had dropped the messenger bag somewhere beside the door, and it took her a few minutes to find it in the dark. She answered and was back at the window, cutting off Jack's greeting. "He's got it."

"The painting?"

"Yes. I'm watching him through my window. It was in the bag. He's set up a desk lamp over the painting and is bent over it right now, examining it. Looks like he's got a jeweler's loupe."

Jack blew out a breath. "That's good. I got nothing, except Anna's hotel." In the background, Zoe heard a car horn and traffic noise. "A five-star place off the Champs-Élysées. She came directly here and went right up to her room. I'm on my way back."

About thirty minutes later, Jack came in the door. "What's happened?"

"Nothing. He's still examining the painting. He's going over it an inch at a time." Jack came to the window, and she handed him the binoculars.

"What's wrong? You shouldn't look so stressed. We found the painting. No orange jump suit for you—or me, for that matter."

"It means we have to get it. How are we going to do that?"

"Unless you have a couple of million in the bank and can buy it from him, we'll have to take it."

"I knew you were going to say that."

"I hate this." Zoe inched closer to Jack, away from the street-light as they left their hotel. They had waited, watching the rooms above the gallery until the light on the worktable went off. Masard's shadow passed back and forth in front of the shutters as he moved from the main room into an adjoining room, where lights clicked on, and finally after about forty minutes, the main lights switched off around ten. Then they waited two more hours to make sure he'd really gone to bed.

"Don't skulk." Jack caught her hand before crossing the street. "We're just two romantics out for a moon-lit stroll on a Paris night. Let's make the block. Don't want to go directly from our hotel to the gallery in case anyone is watching."

"Ouch." The handle of the screwdriver in Jack's palm thwacked Zoe's wrist. "Don't tell me you brought a set of tools along with the binoculars."

"I wish. No, that would raise a few eyebrows at airport security, and we didn't want any extra attention. I borrowed these from the hotel's maintenance closet." Jack fell silent as another couple passed them, their arms entwined.

"I hope he's asleep by now," Zoe said as they rounded the corner and approached the gallery. "This is breaking and entering. In a foreign country. You do know the French don't have the same guarantees of individual rights we do, don't you?"

"Let me know if someone turns onto this street."

Jack bent over the lock in the arched gallery door. Zoe crossed her arms. "They don't have the same due process we do. You remember those paparazzi who were trying to get photos of Princess Di? They were arrested the night she died."

"Where do you get all this?"

Zoe shifted her feet. "A *Celeb Entertainment Special*."

"One of the foremost legal authorities. I always rely on *Celeb* for any legal opinions I need."

"Stop it. This is serious."

"Yes, it is, but you like stuff like this—crazy, impulsive, edge-of-your-seat stuff."

"*Legal* crazy, impulsive, edge-of-your-seat stuff. Believe it or not, I've never broken the law before." She paused. "Well, maybe bent it a bit, but I've never done anything like this."

Jack stood. "Well, fortunately, your impeccable record will stay clean. It's unlocked." Jack pushed the door open and stepped inside.

"Do you think he forgot to lock it when he got back with the painting? Too excited?" Zoe asked in a whisper as she pushed the door closed. They moved carefully through the dark shop. Zoe tucked her elbows in to avoid a painting on an easel and maneuvered carefully around a vase on a pedestal.

"Doesn't seem likely. Wouldn't having a multi-million

dollar painting in your possession make you *more* likely to remember to lock up, not less?" Jack said in an undertone.

"I just hope someone didn't break in before us while we were going around the block." They might not be the only people interested in the Monet painting. Had someone else been watching Anna as well? Had someone been watching *them* as they watched for the painting? Was it Mr. Gray's man? Did he not trust them to bring him the painting? Was it some unknown player?

Zoe edged around a rolled oriental rug propped against a looming armoire. They froze at a noise from above, a scrape of wood on wood, as if someone had bumped a table or chair. There was a muted cry and then a thud.

Jack hit the iron stairs at a run, his feet ringing like gunshots in the quiet shop. Zoe galloped up behind him. The small room at the top was dim, lit only by a single light set into the underside of the upper cabinets in the kitchen portion of the room, which lit up a small area of the cabinet where a teacup lay on its side next to a teapot on a hotplate.

"It's gone," Zoe whispered. The worktable was empty. "Masard's certainly tidy. He's already cleared away the lamp that was on the worktable and the bag the painting was in." Zoe's gaze swept the small room. There were many places where the painting could have been stashed—the filing cabinets and desk for starters. "I hope we can find it. I don't think Mr. Darius Gray is the type of person who accepts failure."

"Before we worry about that we'd better find Masard. Where is he?" Jack asked, matching her low tone. "He was obviously making himself another cup of tea..."

Zoe saw a slipper. "I think he's over here." In the shadows cast from the single light, she could see the form of the pudgy man, face down on the floor on the far side of the worktable.

10

Zoe stepped around the worktable and caught her breath. Masard's face was turned to one side, and his temple rested in a dark puddle that was spreading across the floor and soaking into the robe that was loosely belted around his wide waist. "Oh, God. That's so much blood."

Jack snatched a tea towel and pressed it to Masard's head. It was saturated in a few seconds.

Zoe looked around for something else. She grabbed a throw draped over the back of one of the armchairs. As she tossed it to Jack, footsteps sounded behind her.

Zoe half-turned. A figure wearing a knit ski mask crashed into her shoulder, and the blow sent Zoe to the floor. The figure—head to toe in black and clutching a rolled piece of canvas in one gloved hand—stumbled toward the circular stairs.

Jack lunged for him, grabbed an arm.

Zoe scrambled to her feet. The figure swung around, using his momentum to carry both himself and Jack toward the staircase in a large arc. They slammed into the iron railing. The canvas slipped from the black figure's gloved hand as he and Jack teetered on the top steps, stunned from the impact. Zoe dashed across the room and plucked the canvas from the floor.

The figure in black steadied himself and gripped the railing. He planted a foot in Jack's chest and shoved. Already off balance, Jack reached for the railing, but missed. He disappeared down the steps in a clatter of ringing metal.

Zoe backed away as the masked figure turned to her. For half a second she felt terrified about Jack, but then she heard a string of curses and the solid thud of his feet on the stairs.

Zoe scuttled backward into the kitchen area of the apartment between the kitchen counter and the large worktable. There was nothing on the worktable or the sink that she could reach to fend off the black figure closing in on her. Even the teacup and hotplate were too far away to reach as the figure advanced.

The only thing she had was the rolled painting. *I'm holding several million dollars in my hand*, she thought tangentially. *Can't hit him with that—not that canvas would work as a weapon anyway*.

He lunged for the painting. Jack's footfalls were closer, louder now.

Zoe whipped the painting behind her. She was boxed in. With the kitchen counter on one side and the worktable on the other she didn't have anywhere to go. Even if she managed to squeeze through the narrow opening between the worktable and the apartment wall, Masard's body and the slippery, spreading pool of blood were on the far side of the worktable.

The black figure snatched a handful of Zoe's hair. Her eyes watered as he yanked her head toward him. Through a haze of pain, Zoe stretched her arm with the painting out behind her, putting it as far from the other grasping glove as she could. The reverberation of Jack's footsteps on the iron stairs stopped.

A shrill scream split the air, startling Zoe and the attacker. The tension on her hair eased a millimeter. *It's the teapot*, Zoe realized as the loud whistle continued.

Before he clamped down on her hair again, Zoe pushed her shoulder into the figure's stomach. She propelled him backward, and together they hit something solid. The worktable, Zoe figured as she tried to twist away.

Then Jack was there, too, and there were a few seconds of utter confusion as they struggled, a mass of tangled limbs. The interminable whistle of the teapot continued as they rolled as a unit, squashing Zoe to the worktable. *This is what it must feel like to be trampled*. She felt the rough canvas of the painting moving across her fingertips as the weight of two bodies pressed down on her.

She tightened her grip, at the same time wondering if she was damaging the painting, but she couldn't let the black figure take it. She squeezed her hand tighter around the canvas and yanked it free. "Jack, the painting," she wheezed as she tossed it away from them.

Then suddenly the pressure on her chest was gone. Jack and the black figure had pulled away, still struggling. Zoe gulped air as Jack's fist connected with the black ski mask. The figure fell to the floor and didn't move.

Breathing hard, Jack looked at her as he shook out his hand. "You okay?"

"Um...unbelievably, I think so. Bruised, but not broken. What about you?" Zoe asked, glancing at the stairs. "How far did you fall?" She removed the still whistling teapot from the hotplate and put it in the sink.

In the sudden quiet, Jack said, "Almost all the way to the bottom, but I'm okay. I'll be sore tomorrow, I'm sure." He put a hand to his back. "However, I think that is the least of our worries."

Zoe looked from the crumpled black figure to Masard's prone form. "Assault and battery as well as murder. Yeah, it can't get much worse."

FOR the second time in twenty-four hours, Sato pressed the doorbell on Zoe and Jack's front door and waited. It was a warm afternoon, but the massive cottonwood tree in the yard shaded the front of the house and porch. After a second try, he went around back again and pounded on the door. Deborah had indeed been home yesterday and glad to hear from him. He might call her again, see if she wanted to go to dinner. He was whistling as he cupped his hand around his eyes and looked in the window.

He broke off mid-note. The kitchen looked exactly the same as it had yesterday. No one had moved the dishtowel, added more dishes to the sink, or washed the two glasses and silverware. He turned and made for the house next door. The neighbor informed him that she hadn't seen either Zoe or Jack for several days, but that wasn't unusual. Their paths only crossed when they happened to see each other at the mailbox or when the neighbor contacted Zoe to dog sit. Sato left, already making a list of who he could contact to track down Zoe Hunter and Jack Andrews.

THE wrinkled canvas was on the floor near Zoe's foot. "All for this." She picked it up and set it on the kitchenette countertop.

She turned back to face the room and saw Masard, blood congealed on his face and covering one side of his body, sitting up. She shrieked and took a step back.

"Do not be afraid," Masard said, in slightly accented English. "I was only stunned, not murdered."

Zoe exchanged a quick glance with Jack, who was already moving toward Masard. "No, stay there." Jack put a hand on Masard's shoulder to keep him from standing. "You've lost a lot of blood."

Masard positioned his glasses more firmly on his nose. "I am fine." He struggled to his feet with a couple of grunts, swayed, and reached for the table. "I'll just..." He gestured to one of the chairs near the fireplace. Jack put a hand under Masard's elbow and guided him to the chair. Zoe found some more tea towels under the sink and ran warm water on one. Masard looked like something out of a slasher film. "We need to call 911—or whatever the French equivalent is. You need medical attention."

Masard applied the towel to the gash that ran over his eyebrow. "Later. Later," he said, flapping his other hand.

"No, really. Speaking as someone who's recently been hit on the head, you need to be checked out."

"Soon." He tapped his head. "I am...how do you say it... hard-headed. I will be fine. First, we must take care of the thief."

Zoe shifted uncomfortably, thinking he was talking about her and Jack, but then she realized Masard was gazing with distaste at the black figure still sprawled on the floor. "I'd almost forgot about him. You do think he's just knocked out, don't you?"

Zoe had spoken to Jack, but it was Masard, who replied, "Bah. You cannot hurt that one." He'd wiped his face with the towel and most of the blood was gone from his face but with the gash on his forehead and the blood caked on his robe and the collar of his pajamas, he didn't look like the respectable antique dealer they'd seen earlier. His color was improving, though; he didn't look like a recently revived corpse.

"You know who it is?" Jack asked.

"Of course. It is Alex." Masard pantomimed pulling a mask off his face, and then pointed at the black figure. "Go ahead."

Jack pulled the mask off, revealing a head of blond hair floating with static electricity around a heart-shaped face.

"I hit a girl. Damn," Jack said under his breath.

"Don't feel bad," Zoe said. "She deserved it. I saw her in the street earlier. Nearly ran her down tonight."

Jack swiveled toward Masard. "And she works for you."

"Did. She did work for me. I suspected she was stealing from me, but could not prove it. Until now." Masard shifted toward Jack and Zoe. "And I have you to thank for catching her."

Zoe snorted. "Don't think too highly of us. We're thieves, too."

She could feel Jack giving her a hard stare, but she ignored him.

Masard said, "But not by choice, I think. I heard you mention Darius Gray, no?" At Zoe's incredulous look, he said, "Yes, I heard you talking. After that one," he pointed to Alex, "struck me, I pretended to be unconscious." He shrugged and settled back in his chair. "I, myself, cannot throw the first stone, so I do not look too harshly on you. Besides, you were kind enough to try and help me before that...that slippery one attacked you."

Jack looked down on Alex. "Do you think...she's okay? I hit her pretty hard."

"I am sure she will recover," Masard said. "But check her for weapons while she is out."

"Really? Wouldn't she have used one earlier if she'd had it?" Zoe asked.

"Might not have had time to get it out," Jack said. He bent down reluctantly.

"Here, I'll do it." Zoe stepped around him. She'd never patted anyone down before, but did her best to imitate what she's seen in the movies, running her hands over the woman's arms, legs, and patting her waist. "Nothing," Zoe said.

Alex's eyelashes fluttered, and her head rolled slightly to one side. Zoe stepped back. "She's coming around."

Alex groaned and put her hand to her jaw. The instant she opened her eyes, Masard let out a barrage of French. She did a disoriented sweep of the room, taking in both Zoe and Jack before her gaze ended on Masard. He was still talking, gesturing with his free hand, pointing at her, then to his head. The bloody tea towel was now pressed against his head, except for a few times when he pointed it toward Alex to emphasize his point.

Alex sat up slowly. Jack tensed, but Alex held one hand up, conveying she wasn't going to make a move. Jack didn't relax his stance or look away from her. Alex said something in French to Masard, but he overrode her words. Zoe watched Alex's gaze dart around the room as she argued with Masard until it came to rest on the roll of canvas on the kitchen counter. Jack was positioned between it and her. Masard must have realized what she was staring at, too, because he said something sharp that drew Alex's attention back to him. He waved a hand at the stairs and barked a command, then said in English, "Alex is leaving. Now."

"Is that wise?" Jack asked.

"Yes. She understands her choices."

Alex's eyebrows lowered in a scowl as she got slowly to her feet. She moved stiffly to the stairs and walked down them slowly, each footfall decisive and loud. A few seconds after she reached the bottom, the front door closed with a rattle of glass.

"Dieu merci! She is gone." Masard nodded, a single exaggerated motion of his head, then immediately winced in pain.

"Are you okay?" Zoe asked.

"Yes. If I do not move quickly, I will be fine."

"Are you sure that was smart? To let her go?" Zoe asked.

"Ah, you see it as letting her go. For me, it is getting rid of her, which I have been trying to do for months. She will not trouble me again. I made it very clear that I will be calling the police to inform them of her assault and attempted theft. If she moves quickly, she may be able to get out of Paris before they come looking for her."

Zoe shot Jack a quick look. How could their lot be any different from Alex's?

"What is that smell?" Jack asked at the same moment Zoe caught a whiff of an acrid, smoky aroma.

"Something hot. The hotplate is still plugged in—" Zoe turned to the kitchen counter. "The painting!"

Both Zoe and Jack darted forward. The cylinder of canvas had rolled two inches across the counter and now rested against the glowing coil of the hotplate. A thin line of smoke rose from the canvas.

Zoe got there first and jerked the canvas away.

"Oh, my God." Zoe unrolled the canvas with trembling fingers. An inch-wide hole in the upper right hand corner had been burnt away. The blackened edges of the circle still smoked. "We've ruined a masterpiece," she whispered.

Zoe felt like she was going to throw up and faint at the same time. She dropped the painting on the worktable and backed away. The smell of hot metal and burnt fabric filled her nose.

"Don't worry, my dear," said Masard. "It is only a fake."

"SO you're saying you don't have any idea where Zoe Hunter is?" Sato asked.

"No," Helen said. Sato had caught Helen at work, the county clerk's office, before she left for the day. When he asked if he could talk to her for a moment, she'd led him to the break room, which smelled like microwave popcorn. They were seated at a small round table that had one leg shorter than the other and wobbled when either one of the them leaned on it.

Sato raised his eyebrows at her sharp tone.

She tossed her head, swinging her long gold bangs from her eyes. "Sorry. I shouldn't snap at you. I can't believe she's done it again."

"What?"

"Gone off without telling me where she's going. She's done this before, leaving on the spur of the moment. One of the other times she gave me a story about going to see her mom for Thanksgiving, which I didn't believe for a second, but at least she had the decency to *pretend* she was keeping me informed."

"Why didn't you believe she was going to visit her mother?" Sato glanced at his phone, where he'd sent all the pertinent info on Zoe Hunter. There wasn't much on Jack Andrews. His parents were dead, and he didn't have any close relatives in the immediate area, so Sato was concentrating on Zoe first. "Her mother lives in California?" he asked.

"Yes. Southern California. Perfect place for her."

"Why?"

"You know about Zoe's tween years, right? The reality show? *Smith Family Robinson*?"

Sato nodded. When he and Mort first got the Andrews case, he'd watched an episode of the old reality show about an average family surviving on a tropical island. The mom had been what his dad called a real piece of work—selfish, controlling, and so beautiful that most people overlooked her bad behavior.

"That show gave Zoe's mom a taste of fame and she's like a...I don't know...an addict searching for her next fix. Ever since that show got cancelled, Donna's single goal in life is to get on another reality show." Helen leaned over the table.

"What does that have to do with Thanksgiving?"

"She's a size zero and never celebrates Thanksgiving. She hates 'food holidays' as she calls them. The idea of Zoe going to celebrate Thanksgiving with her is ludicrous."

"Do you have any idea where she might have gone? A favorite vacation spot? Another family member?"

"She has an aunt in Florida. They're close—her Aunt Amanda is her only sane relative, actually. She's a possibility. She's in Sarasota. As for travel, Zoe's never been able to afford a proper vacation. She's traveled recently, but I doubt she can afford a last minute trip to Italy or London. Unless that knock on the head *really* messed her up."

Sato was entering the information about the aunt into his phone, but paused. "I'm sorry, what did you say?"

"Just that it worries me. After the head injury, you know. I'm sure she's fine, and you said you think Jack is with her, so he'll take care of her, but..."

"Head injury?"

"Yes." Helen's eyes widened. "You...didn't know about that? Yesterday, she was injured at a client's house, Lucinda McDaniel's. She was—" Helen broke off sharply.

Sato squinted his eyes. "She was...what?"

"Dead. Zoe said she found Lucinda McDaniel dead. Zoe was hit on the head and knocked unconscious." Helen leaned toward him and the table rocked under her weight. "I know Zoe would only leave town if something was very wrong."

"My thoughts exactly."

11

"You see here," Masard pointed to the land portion of the painting, "the brush strokes are too short." He handed Zoe the jeweler's loupe and motioned for her to look.

He'd retrieved the loupe, the desk lamp, and a large photograph of *Marine* from his desk and positioned them on the worktable. Before he'd assembled the items, Masard had retreated to the other room for a few moments and changed out of the bloody robe and pajamas. He'd returned wearing a pair of light gray pants and a thick sweater over a button-down white shirt. He'd thrown down several frayed towels and mopped up the pool of blood near the worktable. Zoe had offered to help him, but he'd tossed them in a bucket and said he'd call his cleaning lady. They were now all hunched over the painting.

Zoe looked at the magnified brush strokes, focusing on several thick splats of gold, green, and tan then transferred her gaze to the section of the photograph that Masard was pointing at now. She shrugged. "I don't see it." The difference in the size of the painting and the size of the photograph made it hard to judge the length of the brushstrokes. And, truthfully, she couldn't stop looking at the ugly, charred hole in the painting.

"They are different. I suppose you will have to trust me on that, but it is not the only thing. Look at the signature. See the stroke on the letter *C* of Claude? Now look at the photograph. What do you see?"

Zoe squinted at both a moment before saying, "The *C* on the painting has a wider curve than the one in the photograph."

"Excellent!" Masard proclaimed as if she were his star pupil. "The forger was so worried about getting the word Monet exactly right that he—or she—did not work as hard on the first name. But that is not the biggest error." Masard flipped the painting over roughly and a few bits of ash fell to the table. "What do you see?"

"Um, nothing." Zoe wondered if he wanted her to examine the back of the painting with the jeweler's loupe.

"That is right. Nothing!" He sounded as delighted as if he had found the actual painting.

"I'm afraid I don't understand."

"Most paintings have marks on them—stickers, stamps, something of that sort. As great masterpieces move through museums and large personal collections, marks are made on the art itself to keep track of the pieces. Inventory marks, if you will. This painting has been in existence since the late 1800s, moving in and out of collections and museums." He waved his hand over the canvas like a magician about to pull a rabbit out of a hat. "They forgot to forge the back."

"You're sure it is a fake? Absolutely?"

"Yes. There is no question. Not even a very good fake. It would not fool me, or even a less astute expert. Now that we have taken care of that, why don't you tell me how Darius Gray is involved?"

Zoe looked at Jack with slightly raised eyebrows. Could they trust him?

Jack nodded but he lifted his shoulder half an inch, and Zoe knew as clearly as if he'd spoken that Jack was thinking they didn't have much choice. She agreed. One call from Masard to the police, and they were done.

Masard's dark eyes took in the quick exchange between them. "I see you are reluctant to involve me...but I am already involved." He waved at the fake painting then touched the cut over his eyebrow.

Zoe said, "Darius Gray wants that painting—the real Monet. He thinks I have it. Obviously, I don't, or I wouldn't be here now."

Masard said, "And I am sure he provided...sufficient motivation...to make sure you give him the painting."

"You know him, then?" Zoe asked.

"Yes. Unfortunately, a friend was forced to deal with him several years ago. I have managed to avoid him until now. I find his methods...distasteful."

"I agree with you," Zoe said, "but right now I don't have a choice."

"Yes," Masard said. "I am certain he made sure you only had one course of action. He likes to box you in."

Jack had been leaning against the table, arms crossed. "He thinks we're boxed in, but we may have an option to turn the tables on him. However, to put that option into play, we must have the real painting. Will you help us?"

"Find the real painting?" Masard asked with a lift of his eyebrow. He winced as the skin on his forehead wrinkled.

Jack said, "I was thinking more along the lines of you not

contacting the police about us or Anna—that is the real name of the woman who gave you the fake."

"Of course I will not turn you in. What a way to repay my rescuers. Well, not immediately. I can delay before I talk to the police."

It would have to do. If they didn't find the painting in two days, Masard would go to the police anyway. Zoe tilted her head. "*Can* you help us find the real painting?"

"I am afraid my skills and contacts do not reach very far into the world of the black market."

Jack looked at the painting.

"I play about in those waters only occasionally, and only in the shallowest of water."

Zoe frowned. "Handling the sale of a stolen Monet is the shallow end of art crime?"

"I agreed only to look at the painting and make inquiries," Masard said. "There are several different types of interested parties who are anxious to acquire the original painting, including the police, insurance companies, and other interested parties."

Zoe tensed. "You're in contact with the police?"

"No," he waved a hand nonchalantly, "not yet. There was no need to involve them until I saw the painting."

"I see," Jack said.

Zoe thought she understood, too. "You contact the police...occasionally? When it suits you?"

"Stolen art does infrequently come through my shop. I may drop a discreet word to the police at a judiciously chosen time."

"But not all the time," Zoe said.

He shrugged. "A man must make a living." He turned to the sink. "Time for a cup of tea, I think." He filled the teapot and put it on the hotplate again. "A habit I picked up years ago when I lived in England for a short while." He took three teacups and saucers from a cabinet and set them on the worktable. "Please," he said, gesturing to the barstools tucked under the table.

Zoe and Jack took a seat as Masard assembled the tea things. "Back to your problem." Masard placed sugar on the table, removed a lemon from a tiny refrigerator in the lower cabinet and cut several thin slices as he spoke. "I can ask a few questions, but I am not active in that area. It may come to nothing, but we will see."

Zoe rubbed her forehead. "We thought Anna had the real painting. She is still the best lead we have. Even if she doesn't have it anymore." As she said the words, a coldness settled over her. What would they do if they couldn't find the painting? It had been months since they'd seen Anna with the painting. She could have sold it or hidden it anywhere.

"We have to stay with Anna," Jack said.

"Is this Anna an artist?" Masard asked.

Zoe shrugged. "No idea."

"No matter. If she isn't capable of that rather amateur forgery, then she probably hired someone to do it for her. There is a good possibility that she has the original. Much easier to forge a painting from the original than from a photograph. Of course, if the artist was working from a photograph, that might explain the poor quality of the fake."

"Will you contact her tomorrow?"

"No. She was quite insistent that we not meet again. Clearly, she thought I wouldn't recognize the painting is a fake. She gave me the bank account number to wire the funds from the buyer. She expects a transfer tomorrow." The teapot whistled.

"So we have at least a day," Zoe said as Masard removed the teapot from the hotplate and poured tea into their cups with a flourish. She felt a surge of grogginess slipping over her and fought off a yawn.

Something about tomorrow teased at the edge of Zoe's mind...what was it? She fought off another yawn as she felt her body downshifting off the adrenaline high she'd been on. She pushed her shoulders back and straightened out of her slump. What was it about tomorrow that was important?

"Oh! The airline ticket," Zoe said, more to herself than anyone in the room. Wasn't Anna's return flight scheduled for —she checked her watch—it was now almost three in the morning—today? "Anna's flight."

Jack held his hand out flat in a 'keep it down' gesture as he glanced at Masard, who had turned away to return the teapot to the hotplate.

"I will contact her and tell her there was a mix up." Masard returned to the worktable and stirred his tea. "Perhaps a bank employee transposed two numbers on the account number. The wire transfer will have to be sent again." He raised his teacup in a toast. "That could take another day at least."

SATO had left the county clerk's office and was striding to his car when his cell phone rang. Dirk Sorkensov. The Kid was probably calling with baby news. Why didn't he call one of the women in the office? They'd pestered Sato all day, asking if he had any news.

He was tempted to let the call go to his voicemail, but

reluctantly pushed the answer button instead. “Got the cigars ready?”

“What? Ah—no.” The Kid sounded tired and the usual upbeat tempo was missing from his tone.

Sato’s stride slowed. “What’s going on?”

“They’re prepping Sophie for a C-section now.”

“Oh.” Sato wasn’t sure how to reply, so he avoided the topic all together. “How are you holding up?”

“Tired, but I have nothing to complain about. Sophie’s the one who’s been in labor for the last twenty-two hours.”

“That’s rough. So...ah...well, thanks for the update. We’re all...um,” what was the appropriate wish for a woman in labor? Not break a leg. Maybe good luck? “We’re...pulling for you, I mean, for Sophie. I’ll let you go.”

“No, wait.” A ragged breath came over the line. “I’ve been thinking about the case.”

“You’ve been thinking about the case?”

“Beats thinking about Sophie going into surgery, you know?”

“Yeah, I suppose so.”

“Did you run down Zoe Hunter?”

“No. I went back to the house today. Nothing’s been touched. Neighbor hasn’t seen them for days. Looks like she and Jack Andrews might have skipped town.”

“What about bank statements and credit cards?”

“Not in yet.” Sato considered adding the detail about Lucinda McDaniel, but decided The Kid had enough on his mind right now. He’d keep it to himself until he confirmed it.

“Listen, that report on the financials,” The Kid continued. “The more I think about it, the more it makes me think of bread crumbs.”

"Has it been a while since you've eaten?" Sato asked. "You might want to hit the hospital cafeteria."

"I'm serious. It looked too easy."

"So easy it took them months to trace it?"

"That was because of all the personnel changes in that division. You said that yourself."

Sato slid into the car with a sigh and paused with the door open and one arm hooked over the steering wheel. He obviously wouldn't be able to get off the phone until The Kid had his say. "Yeah, that's true," he allowed.

"So, those accounts were hard to find, but not *too* hard. Some digging required, but *not much*."

Sato slowly reached to put the key in the ignition. "Someone wanted us to find those accounts."

"They're like a trail of bread crumbs leading us right to Zoe Hunter."

"I'll have the analyst go over them again. Good catch."

"And *that's* why I got promoted. I'll call you if I think of anything else."

"You just go take care of your wife. I'll take it from here."

12

"Slippery fellow," Jack commented as they crossed the street from Masard's gallery to their hotel, the chilly air sweeping a few strands of hair around Zoe's face. "Let's circle the block again," Jack said. They'd convinced Masard to get the cut on his head checked, and he'd phoned for a doctor to make a house call. The small white car with the words S.O.S. Medecins on the door arrived as they left.

Zoe shook her hair from her eyes and turned her face into the nippy breeze. "Yeah, he seemed helpful enough, and if he really doesn't like Gray, he might be telling us the truth—that he's not going to turn us in, but I'd rather get moving once the Metro starts running."

"I'm with you all the way."

The desk clerk handed over their room keys, barely raising his eyes from his paperwork. "Guests returning at three a.m. must not be that unusual," Zoe said as they climbed the stairs. Each step was an effort. She'd been hyped up, running on adrenaline, but the focused tension had drained away and jetlag was sapping her alertness. Her eyelids felt heavy and she couldn't stifle a yawn.

"Either that or he just didn't care." Jack paused in the hallway outside their rooms. "I'll see if I can get us on the same flight as Anna."

"So you had the same thought as I did—follow her to Naples."

"There's no other choice, is there?"

"No," Zoe said. "But how will we follow her once we get to Naples? She might have a car, and by the time we rent one, she could be gone from the airport."

"I've got an idea..." Jack wasn't able to finish the sentence as his jaw cracked with a yawn. She wasn't the only one feeling the effects of jetlag. "I'll take care of it. We could leave now, but nothing is open. We'd either end up wandering Paris on foot, or circling in a taxi."

Zoe blinked and forced her heavy eyelids to stay open. "I don't think we have enough euros for that."

Jack scrubbed his hand over his face. "Or, we could go to the airport and wait there."

"As much as I want to see more of Paris, I'd actually rather see my pillow right now. Just a couple of hours sleep would help. I don't think Masard is going to call the police on us. He's too delighted with the game of trying to find the real painting. And, he doesn't know where we're staying—he wasn't watching out the window when we left. I checked."

The corners of Jack's mouth turned up. "You're getting good at this stuff."

"I know. Scary."

"So, meet at six?"

"Sounds good."

Jack gave her another quick kiss on the cheek. She

wanted to snuggle into the solid warmth of him, but he pulled away and went to his room. Refusing to analyze her feelings, Zoe managed to set the alarm before she fell into bed.

WHEN Sato returned to the office, he answered the barrage of baby questions. “No news. C-section.”

“Poor lamb,” Marie said, shaking her head as she handed him a message slip. “Took that call for you while you were out.”

“What’s bad about a C-section?”

“It’s surgery. There’s always risks with that. And then you’ve got the recovery. Sophie won’t be able to lift the baby or vacuum.”

Sato escaped before she launched into more details.

The name Jenny Singletarry and a phone number were scrawled on the sticky note. Sato tapped it against his palm. Jenny Singletarry...he hadn’t heard her name since Mort retired. She was a reporter who used to ask Mort for updates on cases. She’d broken the fraud story that kicked this whole investigation off. Quite a coincidence that she’d call today.

SATO slammed the car door and felt the muscle pull in his back again. He rotated his shoulders as he walked up the narrow concrete path to the four-story apartment building where Jenny Singletarry lived. He had returned Jenny’s call and left her a message. She’d called him back while he was taking a call from the analyst who had looked over the financial transactions again. He'd confirmed The Kid's hunch and said, "The new boy is right. These transactions are hinky. I'm digging deeper."

Instead of extending their game of phone tag, he'd decided to stop by Jenny's address on his way home from the office. She ran a successful blog and worked from home, so there was a good chance she'd be in. He'd found the police report on the incident at Lucinda McDaniel's house. He didn't like it. Several airlines had answered the police's inquiries about McDaniel. Her office didn't know which airline McDaniel had taken to Lake Tahoe, only that she was away. The manifests from the remaining airlines should come in today or tomorrow.

Sato trotted upstairs. Of course, Jenny lived on the top floor. He crested the top step and knocked on number 407. No answer. He knocked again then tried the looking in the window technique, but Jenny's blinds were shut tight. He turned away and almost ran into a small woman, emerging off the top step.

She had dark hair pulled back in a ponytail, wore an orange tank top, black running shorts, and carried a water bottle that dripped with condensation.

"Excuse me," Sato said, moving around her to descend the stairs.

"Agent Sato. What are you doing here?"

He stopped mid-way down the first flight and looked back. It took him a second longer to recognize her. Her usual glasses were gone, and instead of her hair hanging straight on each side of her face with long bangs covering her forehead, a thin headband held it back, revealing an oval face with a small widow's peak. The few times he'd talked with her before he'd never really noticed what kind of clothes she wore, but he knew he'd never seen her in anything so revealing as the body-hugging workout clothes, which showed a nicely proportioned figure.

He trotted up the steps. "You called me."

She wiped her palm across her forehead. "You could have called first."

"I did. Several times. This seemed the best way to end the phone tag relay."

She unlocked the door. "You might as well come in. Since you're here."

The door opened into a combined living room and dining room. A futon couch, a tiny boxy television, and a comfortable-looking chaise lounge filled the living room. He stopped short at the dining area, which she'd made into an unusual office. The desk was a flat surface elevated to about waist height above a treadmill. "That's interesting."

"It's called tread-desking. Prevents writer's butt," she said with a grin as she moved behind a high counter that separated the kitchen from the rest of the living area. She refilled her water bottle. "Go ahead, try it out."

He realized his gaze was lingering on the curve of her hip and her toned legs. He stepped on the treadmill and hit QUICK START. The treadmill control panel was set behind the desk. Everything else, the computer monitor, keyboard, phone, and even a printer, ranged around the flat surface of the desk, within arm's reach. He upped the pace until he was almost jogging then tried placing his hands on the keyboard.

"Want some water?" Jenny called over the noise of the treadmill.

"Sure." He hit STOP. "Great concept, but I don't see how you type and run."

"Oh, I save my jogging for the streets. I keep it down to a

brisk walk while I'm working. It's just to keep me moving while I'm writing. I spend most of my day on-line." She handed him a glass of water as he stepped off the treadmill.

"Thanks. Working on your blog?"

"Yes, and I do some freelance website design." She gulped water, then hopped up on one of the barstools that lined the high counter. "So, Darius Gray. What can you tell me?"

He recognized the name. A target of many investigations, he always seemed to stay either one step ahead of the law, or he managed to circumvent it. Sato's eyes narrowed. "Just a minute. You're not assuming I'm going to become your go-to FBI contact, are you? Even if Mort gave you information doesn't mean I'm going to."

Jenny rolled her eyes and he was momentarily distracted by how blue they were. How had he not noticed their deep cobalt color? "Share information," Jenny said. "That's what Mort and I did. We exchanged ideas and information."

Sato snorted. "But just because I was his partner doesn't mean I'm interested in *sharing* information with you."

"You're here, aren't you?"

"But not to answer your questions, I've got questions of my own."

"Such as?"

"Zoe Hunter. Has she been in touch?"

"Let me think." Jenny sipped her water then put it down on the counter, looking like she had nothing more to worry about than doing a few post-workout stretches. "Possibly. If you can tell me about Darius Gray it might help me remember."

Sato moved closer to Jenny. He could see each individual eyelash that fringed her blue eyes. "This isn't a two-way street. You have to answer my questions. I can arrest you, if you don't."

She placed a hand on his chest and pressed, moving him away as she sighed. "Always so touchy." He was so surprised she'd touched him that he let her push him away. No one ever touched him when he was in his gruff tell-me-what-you-know-or-else mode.

She hopped off the barstool and went to the tread-desk. "Have you ever heard that expression you get more flies with honey than vinegar?" she asked as she typed. She didn't wait for an answer. "I normally wouldn't do this, but I'm concerned." She swiveled the monitor toward him and pointed to a Facebook message from Zoe Hunter that read, *Hey, Jenny. Something interesting has happened. Can you look into Darius Gray and let me know what you turn up? Appreciate it!*

Zoe Hunter wanted information about Darius Gray. If she was involved with him...

"You see why I thought we could work together?" Jenny took a Bic pen with a blue lid from a jar near her monitor.

Sato's phone beeped. "Sorry, but I have to take this." He recognized the name on his caller ID, the analyst's manager.

"Hi, Donna. So this got bumped up the food chain to you?"

"Yeah," she answered between chomps on her gum. She'd exchanged her nicotine addiction for Big Red several years ago. "It's another con. A con from beyond the grave, so to speak."

"You always did have a flare for the dramatic. Don't keep me in suspense. I'm in the middle of an interview."

"Is she pretty?"

"Donna."

She smacked her gum. "She's got to be, if you want to get back to it. Okay. Okay. I'll get right to it. You know the guy who set up the big fraud originally associated with this case?"

"Costa."

"Yeah, him. He fixed it so the funds taken in through that scam would be routed through a couple of shell companies and then to a Vanuatu company, Verity Trustees, which cooperated with us in our inquiries. They sent the business filings, which lists Zoe Hunter as the owner. That was as far as our original investigation went, but considering that her name was right there for all to see, I looked deeper. I know there are some stupid people out there, but I doubt that someone who was careful enough to shift the money through four other shell companies without her name would be such an imbecile as to leave it in an account with her name front and center. It's just sloppy."

"Maybe she felt it was well-hidden after the other transfers." A pop and whooshing sound came over the line. "You're not blowing bubbles, are you?"

"I would never do that. So unprofessional." More chomping. "No, I'm telling you I deal with this all the time, and people who want to hide assets don't put their name on anything, anywhere, and they certainly wouldn't set up a company in Vanuatu. A couple of years ago, sure, that would have worked, but not now."

"Where's that?"

"It's an island in the Pacific. It was once a tax haven, but they've changed their laws, and the mega-rich don't find it as attractive now. So, we should have picked up on this the first time, but Costa had so many accounts that we were running down that this one got lost in the tangle of everything else.

This file is like one of those weeds that you pull up, and the root system is three times as big as the plant."

"You're sure it wasn't just an amateur mistake? Maybe she didn't keep up with the news on tax havens and thought it was still a good place to go?"

"Nah. I have the emails that were exchanged to set up the account."

"How did you get those?"

"They're in the file. We were able to get the on-line computer back up of the guy who handled Costa's financial transactions, his hacker-cum-financial advisor. If we didn't have that, I couldn't have made the connection. I searched for the account number, and the emails popped up. Only two emails, but they definitely link Costa with the account and spell out that Zoe Hunter is to be listed as the owner. It's not supposed to work that way, but I bet a little payment on the side smoothed over any questions."

"Okay. Thanks for this," Sato said.

"One more thing. There's only been one transaction since the initial deposit. Verity Trustees paid an invoice from The Flynn Gallery of Fine Art for an Impressionist painting. Twelve million dollars."

Sato ran his hand over the back of his neck. "So now we're looking for a painting?"

"Yep. I'll send you what I have." Another pop sounded, this one louder than the other.

"I looked them up, the gallery. Not my department, I know—but this case has sucked me in. I'm curious. I asked around. The art squad is checking the gallery."

"*Our* art squad?"

"Yep." Sato made a mental note to get in touch with the Art Crime Team, thanked Donna, and hung up.

Donna seemed sure that Zoe wasn't involved in the money transfers, but he still wanted to talk with her. Did Zoe know the paperwork had been manipulated to link her to the account? Was that why she disappeared? Why had she asked Jenny about Darius Gray? Was he involved? And how did Lucinda McDaniel fit into all this? He had to find Zoe Hunter.

Jenny twisted the cap as she leaned against the treadmill railing. "I can help you."

"No, you just gave me all your information," Sato corrected.

She laughed. "No, I mean Zoe trusts me. I got the feeling last time she talked to me that she wasn't too fond of you. Don't get me wrong, I'm not going to sell her out to you, but I might be able to convince her to work with you, or talk to you, or whatever it is that you want with her."

Sato frowned. He didn't like being in anyone's debt. It was cleaner that way. No entanglements, no owing anyone a favor, but he had to find Zoe Hunter, not to mention Jack Andrews.

"So let me get this straight. You're saying if I tell you about Darius Gray, you'll help me find Zoe Hunter?"

Jenny had placed the pen in her mouth and was biting down on the lid. She pulled the pen out. "She's missing?"

Sato automatically assessed the concern in Jenny's voice. He thought it was genuine. "Neighbors haven't seen her in days. No activity at her house for over twenty-four hours. And her best friend hasn't heard from her, which is unusual."

Jenny imprinted her teeth on the pen lid. "Oh, that's not good. If she's mixed up with this Darius Gray guy...well, she wouldn't be the first person associated with him to just disappear."

"THE airport or Anna's hotel," Zoe said, weighing their options as they fed their tickets into the machine and pushed through the metro turnstile.

The first minutes after the alarm had gone off had been painful, but a quick shower had done amazing things for her alertness, and now that there was the promise of coffee, Zoe thought she might survive. It hadn't taken long for her to toss her small pile of clothes in the suitcase and check out of the hotel.

Jack, pulling their single rolling suitcase, pointed to the Concorde metro station on the map. "This one is the closest to her hotel. It will be easier to spot her there than the airport." The Metro ride was short, only a few stops, and then they were climbing to street level. Zoe paused at the top of the stairs, her gaze skimming over the small cars, motor scooters, and bicycles whizzing by the row of stately stone buildings lining the street, looking for a street sign so they could orient themselves.

"Zoe, over here." Jack tugged on her elbow, guiding her along a curved stone wall to an immense oval with two fountains on each end and a large stone obelisk in the center, the rising sun glinting off the golden pyramid at its peak.

"The Place de la Concorde," Zoe breathed.

"Come on, we've got time for a quick look." Jack grabbed her hand, and they darted across the road through the growing string of cars merging. A mist of water brushed over them as they circled the fountain. Water sheeted down from a large bowl, cascading in front of stern-faced

. . .

statues. Near the rim of the lower pool, water sprites held fish that spouted water into arcs back toward the center of the fountain.

Traffic was picking up, crowding the edge of the oval. Car horns hooted and motor scooters accelerated, buzzing through the gaps in the stalled traffic, but Zoe barely noticed as she turned to the obelisk. "I read about this on the plane," Zoe said, walking toward it, her gaze fixed on the deeply cut hieroglyphics that marched up the sides of the granite and the glittering gold inlay on the square base. "It's the Luxor Obelisk. The hieroglyphics are about Ramses II and Ramses III. It was a gift from Egypt to France."

"Quite a gift," Jack said. "Bet the shipping was outrageous."

"It was," she said with a smile. "Those gold inlays on the side describe how it was moved here."

She turned in a slow circle, her smile fading. "Before the obelisk, the guillotine stood here during the Revolution. This is where Louis XVI and Marie Antoinette were beheaded." She felt a shiver run over her as she imagined the spacious area filled with an angry crowd, crying for blood.

"The obelisk is a definite improvement," Jack said.

"I agree." Zoe shifted around and gazed up the tree-lined Champs-Élysées where she could see the sturdy Arc de Triomphe in the distance. Moving in a slow circle, she turned until she was facing the opposite direction, looking at the Tuileries Gardens that led to the Louvre. She caught Jack's hand. "Thank you for bringing me here. Have you been to Paris before?" She'd meant to ask him when they arrived, but she'd been too busy soaking up the sights herself, and she'd forgotten. Jack had traveled quite a bit more than she had. "Or is it one of those places you can't talk about?"

"No, the places I can't talk about aren't nearly as nice as this. This is my first trip to Paris. I'm glad we could see it together."

"Me, too." The words popped out before she had time to think about them, but she realized they were true. There was no one else she'd rather see Paris with.

"Come on, let's find some coffee," Jack said. "There's got to be a place around here with a decent chocolate croissant and espresso."

Jack led them to a side street off the Champs-Élysées and nodded at a hotel with twisting topiaries on either side of wide double glass doors. "Anna's hotel." The bit of the interior lobby that Zoe could see through the doors was all veined marble and plush red carpets. They settled at a café across the street at a table in the back row under the shadow of a burgundy awning and ordered espressos.

After devouring her light, flakey, and still warm chocolate croissant, Zoe finished off her coffee then sat back in her chair with a sigh. "So good. Now, about Anna. What's your idea for keeping up with her once she gets to Naples?"

Jack brushed golden pastry flecks from his mouth. Usually he had the clean-cut look going on with a smoothly shaven face and his dark slightly wavy hair trimmed short around his ears and the back of his neck, but today he'd skipped shaving, and the stubble gave him a slightly rakish air. "Your phone."

Zoe raised an eyebrow doubtfully. "My phone doesn't have any fancy stuff on it. It's about as basic as they come." A no-frills phone was one of the ways Zoe made sure her rather erratic, and often minuscule, monthly income covered the bills. She hit second-hand stores for clothes, happily wore Helen's designer cast-offs, and didn't subscribe to cable.

"You can get texts, right?" Jack had pulled his phone from his pocket and held out his hand for Zoe's phone.

"Yes, and take pictures, but that's about all." She dug it out of her messenger bag, but stopped with her hand poised above his open palm. "You're not going to go MacGyver on me and dismantle it to make some sort of tracking device are you? I really need all the numbers in here. It may be simple, but it works. That contact list is my life."

He grinned, his teeth contrasting against his dark stubble. "No worries. No mullet, nothing MacGyver-ish. You'll get your phone back."

"In one functioning piece?"

"Yes. I promise."

Zoe gave him a sidelong look, but dropped the phone into his hand. His phone had all the bells and whistles. He tapped out a text on his phone, sending a message to Zoe's phone. Her phone chimed.

"That's probably the most expensive text I've ever gotten. International roaming can't be cheap."

He typed a reply on her phone. "It will be worth it." He clicked through the touchscreen on his phone then handed it to Zoe. "Watch that screen. Let's see if this works. Back in a minute." He tucked Zoe's phone in his pocket as he stood.

As he strolled away from the café and turned onto the Champs-Élysées, Zoe switched between watching Jack and the screen of the phone, which showed a map of Paris, zoomed in on their current location. A small red dot mirrored Jack's movements as he walked down the street. When he turned the corner and went out of Zoe's sight, the dot moved down the famous boulevard for a few millimeters, then reversed course. After a few minutes, Jack reappeared holding a small bag. The red dot stopped moving when he settled into the chair across the café table from her.

"Impressive," Zoe said.

"It worked?"

"Yep. What's the range on this?"

"Unlimited as long as both phones are turned on and can connect to a cell signal."

"So now we just have to get it into Anna's possession without her knowing. That means we have to get close to her. Or, one of us does. I vote for you."

Jack removed two hats from the bag, one a large brimmed straw hat, the other a men's driving cap in a hound's-tooth check of brown, tan, and red. "Your choice," he said with a straight face.

"Funny." Zoe reached for the straw hat. "I'm tempted to take the driving hat, since you offered. You're lucky I have too much hair to fit under it." Her hair was her most identifiable feature, and if she could keep it covered, she'd feel slightly better. She gathered her hair into a ponytail and secured it with an elastic band she had in her messenger bag, then twisted it up on top of her head and pulled the hat down, trying to tuck in every stray wisp. It wasn't bright enough to need sunglasses, but she had a pair in her bag, a knock-off of the classic black Ray-Bans, so she put those on, too.

Jack had positioned his cap and had settled a pair of aviator sunglasses on the bridge of his nose. "What do you think?"

"You look like something out of a PBS period drama. All you need is a long scarf and a pair of goggles for your drive to the country house. I don't look nearly as swanky as you."

"You look great." Jack reached out and tucked a stray curl under the cap. Zoe felt herself flush.

Across the street, the hotel doors whished open, and Anna strode outside. The red wig was gone. Anna's own short dark hair, glossy black, swung as she strode to the line of taxis waiting in front of the hotel, her black pencil skirt hugging her legs as her Louboutin's clacked across the pavement. She'd exchanged the camel colored coat for a hip-length khaki explorer style jacket with lots of pockets, which was belted tight around her small waist. She pulled a fuchsia hard-sided rolling suitcase behind her.

Zoe's heart began to pound even though Anna was focused only on the taxi driver. Zoe licked her lips. "Time to go." She picked up the phones.

Jack threw a few euros on the table and grabbed their suitcase handle. Zoe squeezed the plastic of the phones in her now sweaty palms. "Now's not a good time to try and plant the phone."

"No, she's too isolated. We'll do it either at the airport here or when we land in Naples."

They crossed the street, passing within inches of Anna as they moved to the next taxi in line. They were so close that Zoe could hear Anna give her destination to the driver, Orly.

In their cab, Jack leaned forward and pointed to Anna's cab. "Follow it to Orly."

Their driver hit the meter and pulled into traffic behind the other cab.

SATO rubbed his eyes then contemplated his closet—a wonder of dark wood shelving, drawers, and designer suits hanging on rods with at least an inch of space between the wooden hangers. He really should check to see what the weather was like in Italy, but he was too tired. It was after two in the morning, and he had to get a few hours of sleep before his fifteen-hour flight.

He'd spent all evening and half the night running down everything he could find on Darius Gray. Sato had discovered that Gray's name cut through red tape like a pair of freshly sharpened scissors. The Bureau wanted Gray. They'd had him once, and he'd gotten off, so they were happy to agree to Sato's suggestion that he liaison with Italian officials and search for Zoe, who could lead them to Gray. Zoe's next-door neighbor had identified a photograph of one of Gray's men, Oscar Watkins a.k.a. Oscar Brown a.k.a. Owen Brown, as a man she had seen hanging around Zoe's house. For the last ten years, Oscar had worked exclusively for Gray as a sort of chief of staff. If Oscar was involved with Zoe's disappearance, Gray was involved as well.

Even the FBI's Art Crime Team was on board. He had a feeling it was their endorsement that had smoothed the way for him to go to Italy. They'd contacted their counterparts in Italy and notified Interpol. Gray was a customer of the shady Flynn Gallery of Fine Art, which specialized in black market art transfers, and since Zoe had apparently purchased a very expensive work of art from them, the Art Crime Team was all for investigating her and any link she could provide them to Gray.

He grabbed several shirts and ties and added them to his suitcase. Italy. He shook his head as he picked up shoes. He'd seen a lot of things in his job, but that one had surprised him. When Jack Andrews' credit card statements came in, he'd expected them to show hotels and restaurants, either in the surrounding area or one of the neighboring states, not Paris and Italy.

The charges indicated he and Zoe were together. They'd paid for two rooms in Paris and now both of them were scheduled on a flight to Naples. What were they doing? Were they pawns in some bigger game, or were they partners with Gray? He'd done everything he could from here. He hoped he'd find the answers in Italy. He set his alarm, rubbed his eyes again, and dropped into bed.

13

The flight was uneventful, except that Zoe's heartbeat fluttered whenever Anna's head moved. The airline was a low cost carrier with no assigned seats. Zoe and Jack had managed to snag two seats together a few rows behind Anna. Jack—of course—went to sleep as soon as the plane pushed back from the gate, leaving Zoe to fidget and watch the back of Anna's head. After the drink cart came through, Zoe took the sheaf of Anna's emails Carla had printed for her. Zoe had skimmed through most of them on the transatlantic flight, but nothing had stood out then. She kept her head down and read, doing her best to ignore the bursts of turbulence as they crossed the Alps.

A few pages from the end, Zoe found another airline reservation confirmation. "How did I miss this?" she whispered to herself. Anna had traveled to Dubai in January. They were about to land so Zoe woke Jack and told him what she'd found.

Jack rubbed his eyes and stretched. "Anything else about Dubai?"

"Nothing. No hotel reservations, tours, or anything. Why do you go to Dubai? It's not exactly a vacation capital. Or is it?" Zoe asked. About the only thing she knew about the city was its connection to the oil industry.

"It's a business capital and a transportation hub for the region. It could have been a transfer point for her."

"I don't think so," Zoe said. "It's the same pattern as this trip. Fly in one day, back to Naples the next."

"Naples was her departure and return city for that trip, too?" Zoe nodded, and Jack said, "That's good. She's probably living somewhere around here, so we may not have far to go."

They didn't have time to talk more because the plane had landed. There was the usual crush of people standing, pulling bags out of the overhead bins, and the push to get out of the plane. Anna whipped her suitcase out of the overhead bin and scooted down the aisle before they could get close to her to plant Zoe's phone.

The Naples airport didn't have covered jet ways that connected to the planes. Instead, two buses idled at the bottom of the air stairs. They followed Anna to the first bus where she snagged a seat and put her suitcase and leather purse in her lap, then rested her arms on them. Zoe shot Jack an exasperated look.

As the bus lumbered away from the plane, Zoe's phone lit up. She had it set on SILENT, so it wouldn't make any noise if it rang or she got a text, but the feature let her know she had an incoming text. "It's another photo," she said to Jack. Her heart thumped while she waited for the picture to load, and her palm felt slippery on the metal pole she held. She was expecting another photo of Helen, but a picture of her Aunt Amanda filled the screen. Zoe's heart sank. "Not her, too." The photo had been snapped in the produce section of a grocery store as her aunt examined fat tomatoes. Absorbed in her shopping, she wasn't aware of the photographer. She'd tucked her blond pageboy behind one ear and held her wrinkled shopping list and half-glasses in one hand.

The photo disappeared and a message stated she had an incoming call. Zoe exchanged glances with Jack as she answered. "Hello."

"Ah, you picked up. Excellent." The man didn't introduce himself. He didn't need to. She recognized the rapid tempo of the words and the slightly nasal voice. *Oscar* she mouthed to Jack as the bus neared the airport. Jack's lips tightened, and he nodded.

"You've received my messages?"

"Yes."

"Don't sound so testy. They are simply reminders of what is at stake. Additional motivation, if you will. Now, how is it going? Do you have it?"

"Not yet. But we're close. Very close."

"Where are you? Exactly?"

Jack was leaning in, his head tucked next to hers so he could hear too. She raised her eyebrows at him. He shrugged and whispered, "Go ahead. He probably already knows."

"We're in Italy. Naples."

"Oh, bonus points for honesty."

"So you knew we were here?"

"Yes, of course. We're watching you—from afar as it were. Electronically. Can't have you disappearing."

"The airline tickets," Jack whispered. "Probably monitoring my credit card."

"This is working out so well," Oscar continued. "Mr. Gray is on his yacht off the coast of Sardinia. Remember you only have one more day. Call me when you have the painting, and I will tell you where to bring it." He hung up.

They didn't have time to discuss the call because once the bus dropped them at the terminal, Anna was off like a sprinter. She sailed through the baggage claim area. Zoe and Jack dodged through the crowds, barely keeping her dark head in sight.

"What if someone's meeting her here? We won't have a chance," Zoe said as they came through the door into the arrival area.

"Then we'll have to grab another taxi," Jack said as they both paused to scan the crowds.

"There," Zoe said. "Going out the main doors."

"She's lined up to pay for parking. Looks like she's alone. I might be able to catch her. Got the phone?"

Zoe handed it to him. "It's still in SILENT mode," she called after him as he jogged away. "I'll be at the rental cars."

Jack raised a hand to acknowledge he'd heard her, but didn't stop. The rental car counters weren't that far away. She got in line and turned back to watch Jack. He eased down to a brisk walk and waved off a gypsy asking for change near the lines of people waiting to pay for their parking at the machine. Jack slipped into the line directly behind Anna. She had her head down, counting out change. She'd positioned her suitcase behind her left hip.

Jack took some coins from his pocket and when the gypsy moved to ask Anna for money, he dropped a coin. He squatted and retrieved it. If Zoe hadn't been watching closely she would have missed how he quickly unzipped the suitcase a few inches and slipped Zoe's phone inside, then re-zipped it in a fluid motion as he rose.

Anna shook her head at the gypsy, reached blindly

behind her for the suitcase handle and pulled it forward as the line moved. Zoe released a breath. He'd done it. Anna took her position at the machine and dropped in coins. Jack moved to another line, but instead of waiting in the queue, he blended in with a tour group moving toward the airport. In a few seconds, he was beside Zoe.

"Smooth."

"Thanks." He flashed her a smile. "You're up next. You get to retrieve it."

"Let's not talk about that. I'm still shaking from being nervous for you. How can you look so calm?"

"Believe me, my heartbeat is racing, too." Jack checked his phone. "Let's make sure it's working before we get too excited."

They both peered at the screen as the map loaded. The red dot came up. Zoe gripped Jack's arm. "It's moving. Let's get our rental car."

It seemed to take forever for the paperwork, but finally they were done. As they hurried through the parking lot to their car, Zoe tossed the keys to Jack. Naples was his old stomping grounds. He'd worked for the U.S. Consulate in Naples. "You know the streets better than me."

Jack handed her his phone. "You're navigator, then."

The air was balmy and had a hint of humidity, which Zoe knew would make her hair expand as it absorbed the moisture. She was glad she had pulled it back in a ponytail out of her face. In weather like this, she had a tendency to turn into a big-haired 80s look-a-like.

The sunlight was intense, sparkling off the chrome and glass as they made their way through the parking lot. Zoe was glad that she'd worn a sleeveless black shirt with white polka dots. She'd layered on her sweater and jacket that morning in

Paris, but shed them both under the strong sunlight. They tossed their jackets and hats onto the backseat along with the suitcase, did a quick circle of the compact black car to make sure there wasn't any damage, and then they were on the road.

"She's left the airport and is merging onto the freeway, the A3."

"Toward downtown Naples?"

"No, the other way."

"Okay. Interesting." Jack turned onto the narrow street that was both the entry and exit for the airport and plunged into the throng of cars navigating a traffic circle. Completely ignoring a yield sign, a dark Mercedes crowded up against their car, trying to nose in front of Jack. Zoe sucked in her breath at the closeness of the car. Less than three inches separated them.

Jack laid on the horn and forced the driver to give way. He shifted gears and accelerated out of the crush of cars into an open lane. "Ah, driving in Naples. It's almost a contact sport."

"I knew there was a reason I didn't keep the keys."

"Come on. You'd love this. It's kind of like bumper cars."

"This isn't a ride at the fair."

"You need to tell that to the Italians," Jack said, pointing to a dented Fiat that swooped in front of their bumper at the last moment before the entrance ramp to the freeway.

Once they hit the freeway Zoe relaxed a little. The drivers on the freeway weren't as aggressive as the drivers in Naples itself. The only worry seemed to be cars weaving lazily back and forth across the lanes, seemingly oblivious of the stripes on the road. If they veered too close, Jack gave the horn a tap, and they drifted away.

The triangle of Mt. Vesuvius came into view, dominating

the horizon in front of them. It didn't have the traditional mountain peak. The top was flat, a result of the eruption in the first century that destroyed every community in the area, including Pompeii. Ash and debris from the eruption spilled into the bay of Naples, creating the land that they were now driving on.

"Look at the snow," Zoe exclaimed. White coated the top fourth of the mountain. It did snow occasionally in Dallas, but it was rare enough that the sight of it made her smile.

They exchanged a look, and Zoe knew he was remembering their last visit to Naples.

The road curved south, following the arc of the bay, and Zoe twisted around to keep the flare of the mountain slopes in sight as long as possible. "All those years of editing Italy guidebooks and dreaming of seeing Italy. I never thought I'd see Mt. Vesuvius even once. How lucky am I that I've seen it twice."

"Second chances are rare things," Jack said, his gaze on the road, but Zoe knew he was talking about them. She focused on the tracking program on Jack's phone. She couldn't handle a serious relationship conversation right now. "Anna didn't take the exit for Pompeii. She's going south, toward Sorrento."

"Sorrento," Jack said with a smile. "Another thing to mark off your list."

"Do you think we're going there?"

"Not many other places we can end up."

It was true. The Sorrentine Peninsula formed the southern arm of the Bay of Naples with the island of Capri just a few miles off the tip. They had to either be making for Sorrento or one of the villages that lined the southern side of the peninsula along the Amalfi coast.

The road followed the curve of the bay then turned inland, climbing up into the hills, twisting through small villages with red tile roofs and through groves of olive trees. Zoe drank in the scenery, but all the while in the back of her mind was Jack's statement about second chances. He wanted a second chance, but it had gone so bad, so quickly the first time. She didn't know if she could handle that again. Sure, the fireworks between them had been amazing, but that stage had fizzled pretty fast, and then there were only long, tense silences on Jack's part as he threw himself into his business and loud, angry words on her part.

"Look at that," Jack said, snapping her back to the present. The road had crested the hills that lined the peninsula and emerged on the southern side. They skimmed along a sheer cliff, the road switching back and forth in a series of hairpin turns. Above them, scraggly bushes and long grasses grew near the road. Higher up, pines alternated with steep rock faces. Below, the sun glittered on the sea, revealing deep coves and inlets with water a dark navy hue, yet it was somehow also translucent, revealing rocks far below the surface. A few boats bobbed into view as they swept around a turn. It looked as if they were floating on a sheet of blue glass. "What do you have to say?"

"I think I'm speechless."

"I know the feeling."

A bus lumbered toward them on the opposite side of the road, seeming to take up more than its fair share of the narrow lane. Zoe leaned to the right, and Jack downshifted, hugging the low rock wall on their right. The bus whipped by them and Zoe let out a breath.

The road snaked around a rock outcropping and a town came into view. "There's Positano," Jack said. A burst of color, houses in white, yellow, orange, and even red filled a crevasse in the mountains, spilling steeply down the hillside to a golden sweep of beach. The sea, dotted with boats of every size from rowboats to yachts, stretched out sparkling in the sun.

"Where's Anna?" Jack asked.

"Oh!" Zoe checked the screen of the phone, which she'd been holding but had forgotten in her lap. "There she is," she said with relief. "She's left the main road and is in Positano." The red dot traveled slowly along the twisty road, moving deep into the village. "She's going slower."

"We've got to catch up with her in case she stops and leaves the suitcase in the car." Jack hit the gas, and they swooped along the narrow road. White stucco houses with flowering vines trailing down their walls swept by. They flew by shops with hanging baskets of lemons and tangerines, colorful clothes flapping in the breeze, spinning post card racks, and decorative painted tiles. Jack hit the brakes, screeching to a halt for a tour group slowly crossing the road then accelerated again. The road dipped down into the heart of the village, then rose again, winding back up through the far side where it would rejoin the road that skimmed along the coast.

"Wait. She's stopped."

14

"Where? How far are we?" Jack asked.

"No idea. This doesn't show where we are, and we're going too fast for me to see a street sign." Jack slowed. Zoe scanned the area, looking for a cross street with a visible street sign, but she only saw hotels, shops, and restaurants. They were on the outer edge of the village, the buildings clinging to the rising ground, giving good views off back terraces over the town and the sea. There hadn't been many parking spaces in Positano itself. But here there were some slots along the road and a scattering of small paved lots interspersed between the buildings.

Zoe's gaze snagged on a woman with dark hair who'd parked in one of those small parking areas. She rose from a black convertible Porsche, the longer side of her hair swinging against her cheek as she closed the door. "There!" Zoe squeaked. Anna turned and walked down the street directly toward them. She'd removed the belted jacket, revealing a sleeveless black sheath that hugged her curves.

Zoe ducked. She didn't dare look up. Jack slid lower in his

seat and reached up to adjust his sunglasses and shield his face as their paths crossed.

"Did she see us?"

Jack watched the mirror. "Don't think so. She's going into a building." Zoe scrambled up, twisting around in time to see Anna pass a gnarled shade tree and walk under a awning striped in blue and white with the name Hotel Santa Lucia. Jack spun the wheel, slipping into the last open slot in the same tiny parking area.

"Let's stroll," Jack said, handing two euros to the man who monitored the parking lot. The attendant had waved Anna into the restaurant, so Zoe figured if you were eating there you didn't have to pay.

Zoe snatched up her hat from the backseat and tucked her hair under it. They ambled in the opposite direction to a shop across the road with bright clothes fluttering in the breeze as they dangled on hangers hooked to window seals and the doorframe. The warm breeze felt good on Zoe's bare arms.

Inside, Jack picked up a white baseball cap with the words AMALFI COAST. "Don't think the hound's-tooth hat will blend here," Jack said. He paid while Zoe stayed near the shop's front window to keep an eye on the hotel Anna had entered.

The striped awning led to an open-air terrace restaurant with an amazing view of the sea and Positano. A partial roof covered the right-hand side of the restaurant where an arched doorway opened to the hotel's red-tiled lobby. A bar stretched along the wall next to the entrance to the hotel. Anna sat in the shade at the bar, her back to them, talking to the bartender, a young man with a thick head of dark curly hair, who smiled at Anna, his teeth flashing white against his deeply tanned skin as he unloaded a tray of clean glasses.

Jack peeled the price tag off his hat before settling it low over his eyes. "Still in there?"

"Yes. Doesn't look like she's going anywhere soon. She's got a drink and seems to like the bartender."

The bartender set a fresh drink in front of Anna. Jack's gaze traveled from Anna to the Porsche. The top was down on the car, and Zoe could just see a corner of the fuchsia suitcase glowing brightly under the intense sun. "We're close enough now that we can keep her in sight. This might be your best chance to get your phone back."

"*My* best chance?"

"I planted it. It's your turn."

"I knew you were going to say that."

"Unless you want to distract the parking attendant?"

She glanced at the guy with the wrinkled face and the sour expression, who sat on a stool under the shade tree. "I'll get the phone." She wanted to stay as far away from Anna as she could, and they had to get the phone back before Anna opened her suitcase and found it.

"You can do it," Jack said. "I'll ask him directions and pretend I can't understand Italian. We can meet at that little café a few doors up the street from here."

Zoe blew out a breath. "Okay, let's go."

Jack squeezed her arm as they stepped out of the shop. Zoe kept the brim of her hat tilted to cover her face as she crossed the street. Out of the corner of her eye, she watched Jack approach the attendant. She slipped between the cars and hunched over until she reached the Porsche. A few potted plants set along the edge of the parking lot did an ineffective job of screening the view of the cars from diners, and they wouldn't block Anna's view if she looked over her shoulder.

For half a second, Zoe debated opening the door, but decided not to. She didn't want to risk an open door warning ding—or worse—set off the car alarm. Zoe raised enough to reach into the backseat and pulled the suitcase's zipper down. She shoved her hand into the opening and felt nothing but fabric. The phone must have slipped deeper into the suitcase.

Anna's laugh filtered through the air. A bead of sweat trickled down the side of Zoe's forehead as she buried her arm deeper in the suitcase. She dug through slippery silks, rough cottons, a stiff leather belt, and the rather vicious point of a stiletto heel. No plastic. The sour-faced man waved his arms, gesturing like he was throwing a ball down the street. Jack shook his head.

Zoe gave up trying to be subtle. With a quick glance at Anna, who was blowing a long stream of cigarette smoke skyward, Zoe fully unzipped the suitcase and splayed it open on the backseat. She was now standing, leaning into the Porsche, in full view. She kept her head down as she churned through clothes, shoes, and accessories. *It had to be here. Unless...had Anna found it? Had she opened the suitcase for some reason...* Frantically, Zoe patted the side pockets. She felt a rectangular outline and extracted the phone from an interior pocket, at the top of the suitcase.

Zoe re-zipped the suitcase, shoved it back where she'd found it, and slinked away.

Jack joined her at the café a few minutes later. Zoe fanned herself with the menu. "I need a drink. I think I had my first hot flash. It was in a pocket. An interior pocket. How did you do that?"

"I didn't do it intentionally. It must have caught the edge

of the pocket when I shoved it in there. " Jack pointed to the phone on the table between them. "But you got it back. That's all that counts."

"Well, all I can say is that if we have to plant it again, it is definitely your turn. Now where's my limoncello?"

"DO you think she's ever going to leave?" Zoe asked, as she sipped a club soda with a twist of lime. She'd had her limoncello, but Jack had insisted they order lunch with it. The owner of the café recommended the antipasto plate. They had worked their way through the menu from a delicious lamb dish to a noodle and seafood plate.

Zoe's gaze drifted away from Anna to an older lean man with shiny dark hair and a deep tan trudging up the hill. He paused to adjust the blue plastic bag that he hauled on his back like Santa. He held it in place with one hand and with the other he gripped a large piece of cardboard with a space cut away for a handle. The cardboard had all sorts of things attached to it. Sunglasses, snorkels, goggles, hats, and jewelry were spaced evenly across the board and fastened so that they didn't fall off when he lifted it. "Look at all that stuff that man has," Zoe said.

"Street vendor," Jack said. "They sell stuff to the tourists. Usually they walk the beaches or set up on busy streets in town. "This guy is probably headed to catch a bus home, but it looks like he's going to hit us up on his way." The man was moving in their direction, but a car came around the curve from below, moving up the slope of the hill toward him. The man glanced over his shoulder, spotted the car then quickly reversed course, melting into a narrow opening between two buildings.

The gray car with the words, Guardia di Finanza, on the side in yellow slid by slowly, lingering for a moment at the gap in the buildings where the man had vanished. Zoe looked at Jack with raised eyebrows. "Tax police," he said. "The street vendors aren't licensed and don't charge their customers tax, so they don't pay taxes to the government."

"Ah, I see. Thus, the disappearing act." Zoe turned her attention back to the restaurant, but Anna hadn't moved. She still sat at the bar. She'd smoked at least three cigarettes, had several drinks, and a plate of food. The restaurant had a few scattered customers when she arrived, but they'd been served and departed. The bartender mixed drinks and served tables, but had never left Anna alone for long. It was siesta, the time when everything shut down for a few hours in the afternoon, but it didn't look like Anna was in any hurry to leave.

Jack had asked the café owner if he was ready to close, but he'd waved Jack off, saying he stayed open to sell drinks to the crazy turisti who walked the town in the heat of the day.

"She seems quite comfortable," Jack said.

"With the bartender."

"Yes, there is something going on there. Too bad we can't get close enough to hear them."

"No spy gear for long-distance listening?" Zoe teased.

"Wouldn't fit in the carry on," he said.

She shook her head. "And you don't lip read, either. What kind of spy are you?"

"*Was*. What kind of spy was I? All in the past."

"Oh, I think you're doing pretty good now, considering our limitations. No support, and only binoculars and a phone app for equipment." She finished off her lemon pastry with a groan of pure delight. "Now, if we're just going to sit here, I'm going to check email," she said, nodding to the sign on the café window advertising free Wi-Fi.

She removed her computer from her messenger bag and powered it up. Another couple dropped into the seats at the café table next to them and ordered drinks.

"No e-mail. Either for me or Anna," Zoe said. Zoe had been sitting with her ankles crossed, lounging back, managing to feel slightly lazy and full of good food, but when she logged onto Facebook, the soles of her feet hit the ground as she surged upright.

"Kathy updated her status. They're here."

"You can tell that from her update?" Jack asked. "Is there a location tag with it?"

"No. It's in her update," Zoe said, her words quick with excitement. "She says, 'Greece was amazing. Rough night on the *Regent Renaissance* but I can't wait to see the Blue Grotto and Pompeii.' They have to be close."

The woman seated at the table beside them twisted around. "I couldn't help overhearing. Did you guys come in on the *Renaissance*, too?"

"No, but I know someone who is on that cruise. Is the ship close? Naples?"

The woman fanned herself with the plastic café menu, lifting her fine brown hair away from her sweaty forehead. "Closer than that. It's anchored off Capri for the next two days."

The café owner deposited two limoncellos at their table. The man lifted his. "To solid ground."

She clinked her glass against his then swept her hand toward the village. "To wide-open views."

They sipped their drinks then the woman raised her

glass, pointing at the hotel across the street. "That one looks nice. We should check there." The man agreed and the woman shifted back toward Zoe and Jack. "Are you staying in town? Can you recommend a good hotel? I'm Isobel, by the way."

Zoe and Jack introduced themselves, said they didn't have a hotel, and didn't know any to recommend. They chatted a few minutes and learned that Paul was a pharmacist and Isobel was a history teacher. They were from Mesquite, Texas, and this was their first cruise.

"First and last," Paul said, finishing off his drink.

Isobel nodded. "Amen to that. All our friends love cruising, so we figured we'd save up and go on a Mediterranean cruise—what could be better, right? I love history, and Paul loves to eat, although you couldn't tell by looking at him." She gave him a quick pat on his bony shoulder. Zoe guessed Paul was in his late fifties and that his hair had probably once been light blond, but the sun glinted off more silver strands than gold. "I love food, too," she said. "But that's no surprise." While Paul was tall and thin, Isobel was shorter and plumper, filling out the loose caftan-like linen dress she wore.

"Turns out Paul is prone to seasickness," Isobel continued, "and I had no idea I hate small spaces. Our room..." She shivered, sending tremors through the pale yellow fabric of her dress, "it's about as big as a coffin, and each day it seemed to close in on me more." Isobel took another sip of her drink. "I mean, how would we know these things? I'd never been anywhere so confined."

Paul winked at her. "We just like wide-open, landlocked places."

Zoe leaned forward. "I need to get a message to someone on that ship, but he's not checking email or answering his phone. Could I impose and ask if you'd mind taking a message to him when you go back to the ship?"

"Oh, we're not going back to the ship," Isobel said.

"I'm sorry. I must have misunderstood. I thought you were going to stay here for a night and then go back to the ship."

Isobel hitched her chair closer to Zoe. "No, we decided when we came ashore here in Positano. No more ships."

"Or islands," Paul inserted.

Isobel smiled at him. "No islands. No more boats, even short trips. That's what we agreed on. We're staying overnight here in Positano. Tomorrow, we'll go to Pompeii and Herculaneum—its ruins are supposed to be even better than Pompeii's—and then we'll drive up to Rome and catch our flight home."

"But what about your things...your luggage?"

Isobel waved a hand. "It's only a few days. We'll buy a couple of things. We'll meet the ship in Rome and get our stuff then, but if you want to get a message to the ship, I'm sure you can." She picked up a blue ID card that hung around her neck. "Just look for someone wearing one of these." It was an identification tag with her photo and name on it. She pulled it over her head and dropped it on the café table. "Won't need that for a few days."

Zoe had seen a few people wearing the lanyards as they watched tourists stroll by the restaurant. She glanced around, but the street was empty now in the heat of the day. Jack touched Zoe's hand, his gaze on the restaurant. She had been so focused on the couple beside them and possibly getting a message to Mort that she'd forgotten about Anna.

Anna was leaving the restaurant with the bartender. He had his arm around her waist as they strolled to her car. Anna took the driver's seat and the bartender settled into the passenger seat.

"Time for us to move on," Jack said as the Porsche backed out.

"Hope you have a wonderful time on the rest of your trip," Zoe said.

"You, too," Isobel called as Paul touched the brim of his hat with two fingers.

Jack had already settled the bill, so they crossed the street to their rental car and took off down the single lane behind the Porsche.

15

Jack stayed back far enough from the black sports car that they wouldn't notice them as they trailed Anna along the twisty road as it climbed back to meet the main road. Once back on the slightly wider road that hugged the coast, Anna turned left and they retraced their earlier route, whipping along the hairpin turns in the direction of the tip of the peninsula.

"Are you worried she'll spot us?" Zoe asked.

Jack shook his head. "No. There's enough traffic that I don't think we'll stand out." Buses, cars, and motor scooters swooshed back and forth on the sweeping turns, providing camouflage for them until they turned off the main road and entered a small village away from the coast, which wasn't nearly as scenic as Positano. Here, corrugated steel covered shed-like buildings. Instead of the bright white stucco of the villages by the sea, these homes and buildings along the narrow road were gray and plain. No bright tourist wares here.

Jack dropped back in the quiet narrow streets. They took

the wrong road when it separated at a *Y* intersection. When it petered out into a dirt trail, Jack put the car in reverse, and they backtracked to the *Y* then took the other road.

They threaded through terraced olive groves and then the quiet road rejoined the main road with its smooth blacktop and clear white lane stripes. Jack pointed to a flash of a shiny black bumper disappearing around a curve. "There they are. That must have been a shortcut only the locals know."

The road curved higher and there was less traffic here, so Jack kept a good distance back. The road snaked higher and higher toward the rocky white cliffs. They zipped through a little town, white rock walls on either side of the road.

The black car slowed, and Jack dropped back, following it through a quaint town with white stucco walls, a couple of stores and homes, some of them seeming to be carved into the rock of the mountain. The Porsche stopped short at a garage door set into the wall on the cliff side of the road. The glossy wood garage door had a well cared for look that contrasted sharply with the cracked stucco that had fallen away from the wall, exposing the stones. A mass of vines and scrub bushes grew along a trail above the wall, their vines and roots dangling above the open garage door. The engine revved, and the car slipped into the tiny space, stirring the trailing greenery.

Jack zipped by the garage, made a quick three-point turn and whipped into a narrow parking space, hugging a low wall on the side of the sea. The slot was probably for a motor scooter instead of a car, but Zoe figured it didn't matter because there was an even bigger car wedged into the parking place in front of them.

Anna and the man came out of the garage, and it closed smoothly behind them as they backtracked a few feet then turned onto the dirt trail that ran up the hillside directly over the area where the garage was set into the hillside.

The man held Anna's suitcase, and their arms were around each other's waists. The trail paralleled the road, but rose steadily. They watched Anna and the man until a copse screened them from view.

"They looked cozy," Zoe commented.

Jack opened his door. "We'll have to follow them on foot. There's no road up there." Zoe repositioned her hat and stepped out of the car.

A sign at the foot of the trail had symbols of a hiker with a walking stick, a mountain, and a set of wavy lines, and declared they were headed for Baia di Jeranto. "Looks like we're hiking," Jack said. "I remember hearing about this trail when I worked in Naples. It goes all the way to a small secluded beach. The trail is the only way to reach it. Supposed to be amazing. Views of Capri and everything. I wanted to come down here and hike it, but never got to do it."

"How far is the beach?"

"About a twenty or thirty minute hike, I think. One of the guys at the consulate told me about it."

"Well, I don't think Anna's going that far, at least, not in those heels."

"Maybe he's going to carry her," Jack said as they crossed the street to the trail.

"She certainly didn't look like she'd object."

They fell silent as they entered the tree-shaded portion of the narrow trail, which rose steadily. Dry yellow grass grew between flat white rocks that formed a wall higher than Jack's head on their right, while a fence of wooden poles and wire lined the edge of the trail where the ground sloped away on the left. Vines dripped over the fence and the trees touched overhead, but they didn't completely block the light. Sun dappled the trail, flicking over them as they moved. The climb wasn't extremely steep, but Zoe felt sweat gathering around the brim of her hat.

As they emerged from the green tunnel, Zoe caught her breath at the view. They could see for miles along the coast, the green land dropping down to the sea in some places in a smooth curve, in others, a jagged, sheer drop. "Is that the beach?" Zoe asked, nodding at the bay with sunbathers and umbrellas on a stretch of sand and rows of boats bobbing on the sparkling water.

"No, too crowded. And, Jeranto is in the opposite direction."

Zoe was about to comment on the view, but a throaty laugh floated back to them, and she snapped her mouth shut. The view was so stunning she'd forgotten about Anna for a second.

She and Jack exchanged glances. They moved through the small break in the trees and reentered the green tunnel of trees and rock, moving cautiously. They paused at a curve in the trail and watched as Anna and the man entered a gate set in the wire fence.

Zoe edged forward, leaning around Jack's shoulder. From their vantage point on the high trail, they could see down into the small rectangle of land with a villa set into a terraced portion of the sloping ground. A gravel path led from the gate through olive trees to the small, white-washed villa. It couldn't be more than two or three rooms. Blue shutters framed square windows set in thick walls and a flagstone terrace enclosed the house on the three sides away from the path. Huge pots of flowers and vines edged the terrace. Several lounge chairs and a round iron table sat on the flagstone terrace at the back of the villa.

Shadows moved back and forth in front of the windows, then...nothing. No flickering movements in front of the windows. No snatches of conversation. No footfalls.

A bird called in the trees above them. "Siesta?" Zoe asked.

"I'll bet," Jack said with a smile.

Zoe tensed at a scuttling sound at the edge of the trail. A lizard disappeared into the undergrowth.

"Come on," Jack said, reaching for her hand. "Let's find somewhere a little more protected to wait."

They gingerly explored the area around the villa. They settled on the far side of the gate where the trees again enclosed the trail. The ground dropped off too steeply from the flagstone terrace to go around the back, and the right-hand side of the trail with the rock wall rose straight up to a narrow, crumbling ridge with a few scrub bushes.

"This is a good spot," Zoe said, settling on a tree root a few feet off the trail. "The trees and undergrowth will screen us from any hikers, and when Anna and the guy leave, they won't go by us." She took off her hat and wiped her forehead and the back of her neck. "Did you bring your binoculars?"

"Sadly, no. I've learned my lesson. I'll always carry them on me from now on."

"Along with a screwdriver?"

"That, too."

The minutes ticked by. Zoe counted each one of them. She couldn't help checking her watch. She'd never been good at waiting, and this was killing her.

Nothing stirred at the villa.

A few hikers trudged by them returning to the village from the beach, but Zoe and Jack were well back from the path and lower down on the sloping side. They held themselves motionless and none of the hikers looked their way.

The light shifted as the sun glided lower, and the skinny shafts of light filtering through the leaves inched across the ground. After an hour, Jack had slipped away and moved as close to the villa as he dared, but with only a few rows of olive trees in the front, he couldn't get close. "Can't see a thing." He dropped down beside her, his back propped against the tree trunk. "I hope they're not in for the night. I'd rather not explore the house with them sleeping in it."

"He'll have to go back to work. This is just the siesta." Zoe fanned herself with her hat. They were in the shade, but there was no breeze.

"He could be off for the day."

"Don't say that. We've got to find out if the painting is in there." Zoe glanced at her watch and again counted off the days in her mind. Had it really only been two days since Oscar showed up and turned her life upside down? She had until tomorrow. "The painting has to be there. If it's not...I don't know what I'll do."

"One step at a time." Jack had been twirling the stem of a leaf between his thumb and index finger, but he tossed it aside and reached for her hand. He slid his fingers slowly along her palm then laced his fingers through hers. There was something deliberate and intense in his motions as if her hand were something delicate and precious. How could holding hands feel so...intimate? His thumb traced lightly over the back of her hand, sending out little sparks that traveled up her arm and made her feel shivery despite the hot day.

Zoe pulled her hand away. "Jack, you've got to stop this."

His hand hung suspended in the air a moment, then he

dropped it to his lap. He tilted his head and watched her from the corner of his eye. "Why?"

Zoe swallowed. Her throat felt thick. She wasn't choking up, was she? No, she wasn't. She couldn't let this go on. It wasn't fair to Jack. "It's not going to happen. You and me. Again. It's not," she said as emphatically but as gently as she could.

His expression shifted, and he turned his head away, gazing out over the villa. "All right, if that's what you want." He looked back and his gaze was shuttered and distant.

"It's not you," she said in a rush. "You're great. Now that we've got all that secret life stuff out of the way, you'd be wonderful. It's me. You know how useless I am. I'm impulsive and flighty. I'd be a terrible wife. I *was* a terrible wife. You know that. You know what happened last time."

"That's a lie," he said, his voice quiet, but firm. "You're afraid."

It took her a second to process his words. Afraid? Her? She was *never* afraid. "That's absurd. I told you. I'm not good...wife material. You were there last time. You know what—"

"You're scared to trust me. That's what it all comes down to." He looked away, down at the dirt at their feet as he spoke. "You've never really trusted anyone."

"That's crazy...and...wrong," Zoe sputtered, feeling a white-hot twist of fury surge through her. It wasn't only the words, it was the way he'd said them—clinical and detached. "What about Helen? I trust her."

"But you don't, do you? Not really." He looked at her out of the corner of his eye, his gaze assessing, almost daring her to contradict him.

"I wanted to call her and tell her about Oscar before we left, but *you* convinced me not to."

"You only wanted to call her because you were backed into a corner and worried about her safety. You didn't tell her about Lucinda's body going missing. And I know you didn't tell her what happened in Italy. Sure, you told her eventually, but only when it was all going to come out anyway."

"I didn't want to lie to her."

"But by not telling her, you were lying to her. At least, that's how you saw it with me and my past. What did you call it? Lying by omission, I think."

"I can't believe you're saying this."

"I can't either, but I think I understand you now," he continued in that subdued, rational voice. "This free spirit bohemian thing you've got going…that lets you keep everyone at arm's length. You don't have to trust anyone. You can't get hurt that way. I understand part of it is the way you grew up. Your mom is something else, and she's warped you, taught you that the only person you can depend on is you."

"So this is—" Zoe realized her voice was loud and kind of screechy. She forced herself to breathe and start over. "This is my mother's fault?"

"No. She set you on a course. You're following it all on your own now." A note of sadness mixed in with his measured tone cut her more deeply than if he'd yelled. She felt as if his words had slashed across her, leaving raw and painful gashes.

Zoe blinked to clear her wavy vision. "You're just saying all this because I hurt you."

Jack rubbed a hand over his face, leaned back against the tree trunk, and tilted his gaze up to the leaves overhead. "You're right that I'm hurt. I took a risk. That's what happens when you get close to people. You open yourself up." He blew out a sigh. "Zoe, you think you're all about being carefree and living on the edge, but you're fooling yourself. It's all an illusion. You're playing it safe."

Zoe opened her mouth to fling back a retort, but a sound came from the villa. Anna clacked across the flagstones, still in her heels and dress, a trail of cigarette smoke wafting behind her. "Giorgio," she called impatiently, her voice floating distinctly up to them. She stood with her arms crossed, staring at the view, one hand moving the cigarette to her mouth with each drag. The young man appeared, a cell phone at his ear. She tossed the cigarette away and they went back through the house, up the gravel path to the gate, and back along the dirt trail toward the village.

16

Zoe and Jack waited a few beats after Anna and Giorgio disappeared down the trail. Jack stood. "Let's go." His voice was steady, matter-of-fact.

Zoe was boiling for a fight. She wanted to rebut everything he said, but she forced those surging thoughts, her stinging arguments, down. *Later*. She would deal with him later. Right now, it had to be about the painting. "Right."

They dropped down directly through the slope into the garden area with the olive trees. No fence enclosed the sides of the villa, just the one along the trail. Jack gave her a hand down a steep portion. His touch was impersonal, almost clinical as if he were a doctor, checking her pulse. Later, Zoe reminded herself. She'd eviscerate him later. They circled around the back and approached the villa across the flagstone terrace.

A set of double doors stood wide open, and Zoe and Jack passed into a living area. The exterior of the villa was old, the small windows and irregular lines of the building gave away its age, but inside the whole thing had been gutted and updated in a contemporary style. The furniture was squared off and done in shades of white, cream, and beige. A fireplace made of the same white rocks that lined the trail took up one wall. The kitchen, jammed with stainless steel, granite, and every modern convenience, filled one corner of the room. The art on the walls was contemporary and abstract, mostly gray with a few streaks of color.

"Who would want to live in a place with furniture the color of oatmeal?" Zoe muttered to herself. She walked a quick circuit of the room. "No painting here."

"Not in plain sight, no." Jack moved to a sleek storage cupboard on a wall near the fireplace.

"I'll check the other rooms." Zoe headed down a short hallway. The first room was a bedroom with an attached bath. It was decorated in exactly the same style as the living area. Zoe zipped around the room, but except for the pink suitcase flung open on the floor and a mass of clothes, handbags, and shoes popping out of a closet, there was nothing interesting. She dropped to her knees to check under the bed, but it was the type of bedframe that sat directly on the floor. She examined the lone piece of art on the walls, an unframed canvas painted gunmetal gray with a single, off-center neon green handprint. Nothing behind it on the wall or tucked into the back of the canvas, which was a single layer, stretched taut.

Zoe glanced at a hall bathroom—nothing special except the plushness of the putty-colored towels. The last door was closed. The knob turned easily in her hand. The door swung open, and the smell of turpentine wafted over her. She stopped on the threshold, blinking. "Jack."

It was an artist's studio. Canvases ranged around the room, some on easels, others stacked against the walls. A jumble of art supplies—paint, brushes, and rags—covered a flimsy card table in one corner. More glassed double doors led to the flagstone terrace with the view of the sea, but these doors were closed.

All the paintings on the easels were angled away from the door to the room and toward the double doors, probably to get the best light, Zoe thought as she hurried into the room, a feeling of elation buoying through her. *It's here. It's got to be here. It's going to be okay. I'll get the painting, and we'll—*

Her thoughts jerked to a stop as she saw the front of the paintings.

They were *all* the Monet painting. Every painting in the room, she realized as she turned and scanned the canvases propped against the walls, was *Marine*. The curve of the blue sea enclosed with a sweep of brown land was repeated over and over again. Some of the paintings were on canvases stretched over wooden frames; others didn't have a frame and were clipped to large pieces of cardboard.

Jack stopped in the doorway, a look of relief washing over his face, as he saw the canvases, but then the truth hit him, too, as he moved into the room.

"It's kind of a good news, bad news situation." Zoe squinted at one painting.

"I'll say." Jack rubbed his hand over his mouth as his gaze flickered over the room. "There's got to be thirty, maybe fifty paintings in here."

An anomaly, a canvas without the brown beach and blue water, caught Zoe's eye. It was propped against one of the walls with other paintings almost covering it. Only the edge, which was covered with short, bold strokes, was visible. "What's this?" Zoe pulled it out. Monet's signature was repeated over and over across the surface. She spun to show Jack. "He was practicing."

Jack looked over his shoulder. He had squatted down and was flipping through a stack of canvases.

"You think the man—Giorgio—is the painter, not Anna?"

"I don't know. I suppose Anna could be a painter. Although, it seems kind of a messy hobby." Zoe scanned the heap of art supplies. "She seems to wear only designer clothes. I don't see a smock or painting clothes in here, and I didn't see any paint-streaked clothes in the bedroom."

"Any men's clothes at all?"

"I didn't notice any, but I wasn't looking for that. I was concentrating on the painting."

He leaned the canvases against the wall. "I think most of these are practice runs, too."

"Warm-ups?" Zoe put the canvas back and looked at several of the paintings lining the floor. She tilted her head as she moved along the line, trying to match up what she was seeing with her memory of the photograph Masard had of the original Monet painting. It only took a few seconds of studying them for the errors to jump out at her. "You're right. This one, the curve of the bay is wrong—too U-shaped. This one, the colors are off—too muddy...or something." She tilted her head as she switched to study one of the paintings on an easel. "He's getting better. This one is very close. In fact," her heartbeat began to pound, "this might be the real Monet."

Jack stood to the side, his arms crossed, frowning at the painting. He leaned forward, touched a corner, and his fingertip came away with a daub of brown paint. "Don't think so." He crossed to the card table and wiped his hand on a rag. "I think that means you're right. Giorgio is the painter. Anna has been gone for at least twenty-four hours. That paint is fresh. With heat like this, if Anna had painted it before she left, the paint wouldn't be slick to the touch. It might be tacky, but not wet."

Zoe nodded. There was no air conditioning, no vents or individual cooling units for the room. The old thick walls would keep the villa somewhat cool, but once the heat of the day hit, the villa would heat up. It was probably why Anna and Giorgio had left the doors open when they left, to catch the cooler evening breeze.

Zoe leaned in, touched the corner, experimentally. "But why would he paint another *Marine*? Masard let her think he'd fooled her. She thinks she's sold the fake." Zoe paced to the double doors. "Maybe she knows Masard wasn't taken in? But then again, she certainly didn't act like a woman who had been found out. She seemed relaxed. She lingered at the bar and had food and drinks."

"Champagne."

"Really? I missed that."

"They toasted each other, too. It was when we were talking with the other couple, the one from the cruise ship."

Zoe walked back to the easel. "Bubbly. Toasts. New painting," she murmured to herself, then turned slowly to Jack. She could see the same thought had struck him, too. "It's a scam."

He nodded. "Dubai. Their goal isn't just to sell a Monet and get the money. It's to sell the Monet *over and over* again."

"I suppose it could work if the various buyers don't get wind of the other sales." Zoe was examining the paintings on the other easels. "This one is wet, too. And what are the buyers going to do, if they find out they've been scammed? It's not like they can go to the police."

A husky laugh floated through the air. Zoe was bent over

another canvas, her finger poised to touch the paint, but she froze. "That's Anna."

Jack had already moved to the small window set in the wall facing the gate. "I should have followed them, made sure they got in the car. They're almost to the gate."

Zoe looked over his shoulder. Anna and Giorgio ambled along the trail. Anna was smoking again. Giorgio held a pizza box. "They went out for pizza? Couldn't they have gone to a fancy dinner? That takes hours in Italy."

"I'll delay them. You find the real painting. Meet me at the tree where we waited earlier."

Jack was gone before she could stop him. "Find the real Monet," she muttered as she turned back to the room. It was impossible. There were too many, and she was no expert. She needed Masard. She swallowed as she glanced out the window. Jack was hunched over, moving through the olive trees to the gate. Giorgio's phone rang, and he stopped about twenty feet away from the gate. He handed Anna the pizza box then pulled out his phone.

Zoe turned away from the window. Okay. *Think*. She had less than a minute to figure it out before she had to get out of the villa. She hurried to the front of the room.

There were so many. *Too many*. She let out a shuttering breath, her hands pressed to her cheeks. It couldn't be one with wet paint. It probably wasn't propped up along the wall. Surely, if you had an original Monet painting you wouldn't put it on the floor.

An original. The words seemed to reverberate in her head as a movie played in her mind of Masard flipping the fake painting over. Zoe surged to one of the canvases with dry paint and turned it over. Nothing. Blank. She moved to the next one, her hands shaking.

She heard a rattle and a curse. Out the small window, she could see the top of Giorgio's head above the gate. The wooden panels of the gate flexed under pressure, but a flat rock wedged into the crevice at the bottom of the gate held it shut. Zoe caught a flicker of movement at the corner of the yard as Jack slipped through the olive trees and scrambled into the cover of the forest on the opposite side of the yard from where they'd waited earlier.

Don't watch, she muttered to herself. Focus. She lifted a canvas clipped to a piece of cardboard on the easel positioned in the center of the room and saw markings, stamps, and a tiny curling sticker. She dropped the canvas as if it had burned her. *This* was *Marine*, a genuine Impressionist painting by Claude Monet.

The wood on the gate groaned, then the whole fence shook as Giorgio banged on the gate.

Zoe grabbed the painting, replaced it with another version that wasn't on a wooden stretcher, but clipped to a piece of cardboard.

She was almost to the door when a thought struck her. They needed one of the fakes, too. If they were going to make accusations, they needed to be able to show what Anna and Giorgio were doing. She put the painting down at the glass door and scurried back to grab one of the fakes. She went for another one that was clipped to a piece of cardboard. She checked the paint. It was dry. Next, she flicked it up and saw that the back was blank.

As she turned back to the double doors, she caught a glimpse of Giorgio climbing over the fence. She didn't linger to watch. She would have liked something to put the paintings in, a bag or something, but there wasn't anything handy, and she didn't have time to go back through the house.

Gingerly holding the paintings, she slipped out the double doors, closing them softly behind her, and crossed the patio. She peeked around the corner and saw Giorgio pulling at the rock wedged below the gate. Anna must have been standing directly behind the gate because Zoe couldn't see her. While Giorgio's back was to her, she shot through the olive trees and scrambled up the slope, trying to keep the paintings up and away from the dirt, all the while expecting to hear a shout aimed at her.

She crested the rise and slipped into the trees. The sun was much lower now and the area under the trees was gloomy. She tripped on a root and caught herself, keeping the paintings tucked into her side. She reached the tree where they'd waited, but Jack wasn't there. "Jack," she whispered, her eyes narrowing as she studied the various shades of darkness.

She turned back to the villa. The slight rise of ground she was on let her see both Giorgio as he finally removed the rock, stumbling backward, and Anna as she took a last drag on her cigarette and tossed it onto the trail before going through the gate. Zoe zeroed in on a movement beyond the olive trees on the opposite side of the villa from her. It was Jack, crouched down behind a clump of low-growing shrubs. Once Anna and Giorgio moved onto the gravel path toward the villa and had their backs to him, he moved to the trail, avoiding the gravel. Zoe mirrored his movements, traveling slowly through the trees and underbrush trying not to make any noise as she inched toward the trail. She smelled smoke. Someone must be having a campfire, she thought.

But then she saw a flickering glow travel up the rock wall that lined the trail as a flame spread through the dry grass interwoven between the rocks. Struck immobile, she watched, horrified and amazed, as the flames spread sideways across the rock wall and upward to the scrub along the ledge. The flames quickly licked at the leaves of a few low trees, then surged along the limbs that arched over the trail.

She had to move, she realized. If she didn't she'd be trapped on the far side of the flames, cut off from the trail to the little village. Not caring how much noise she made, she crashed through the undergrowth and emerged onto the trail. What had once been a leafy tunnel, was now flaming hot.

She could do it. Just dash down the center of the trail. She took a few steps, but faltered when heat hit her face. Smoke was everywhere now. She heard sirens and saw movement. Shouts sounded from Anna's villa. Calls to turn on the water.

A water hose wasn't going to be enough.

The fire was spreading through the trees, closer to her. She could see Jack through the smoke and flame, waving her back, calling something to her.

"...beach...meet..."

She coughed as smoke drifted, blocking him from view. Ash and tiny embers floated in the air. She waved them away as she backed up. It was too intense. She couldn't get through. She turned and ran, searching for fresh air.

17

Zoe dropped down onto a rock, breathing heavily. The air here was clear and fresh. No smoke or bits of drifting ash. She carefully positioned the two canvases against the rock then wiped the sweat from under the band on her hat as she looked over her shoulder at the trail. The fire must be under control. The thick billowing clouds of smoke that had enveloped her as she ran away from the villa were gone. Now, only wisps of gray drifted over the trees.

Should she go back? Once she'd stopped running after her initial burst to get away from the flames, she'd considered it. She looked down at the canvases propped against the rock. The area would be crawling with firefighters and other official personnel. The trail was probably blocked. How would she get through? A disheveled woman toting two Impressionists paintings wouldn't exactly be inconspicuous. She'd have to go right by Anna's villa, too. She reviewed the topography in her mind, trying to figure out a way she could move around the villa without using the trail, but there wasn't a way to do it. The ground behind the flagstone terrace dropped steeply. She couldn't go that way, and the other side of the trail had been engulfed in flames. No way was she going to try and pick her way through recently charred land. Assuming she could somehow stay on the trail and sneak through the fire-damaged area and avoid notice, she had no idea if Jack was still in the village. He'd motioned her on, and she'd clearly caught the word beach, so chances were that he wasn't even in the village. He was probably making his way toward the beach now.

Probably.

You're scared to trust me. That's what it all comes down to. His words echoed in her thoughts.

She shook her head and quickly stood. There was no going back, at least not now. She had to press on to the beach, and hope that Jack came through. She wiped her hands on her jeans before picking up the paintings. She was trying to be as careful and as gentle with them as she could, but a hike on a dusty trail wasn't exactly ideal conditions for handling multi-million dollar art.

Tucking the paintings into the crook of her arm, she resumed walking. The trail had left the forested area and twisted up to a high, open ridge with low-growing hearty scrub trees and grasses and amazing views with the Gulf of Naples on one side, the Gulf of Sorrento on the other, and Capri straight ahead, if she squinted into the sunset.

She passed a square watchtower built on one of the promontories and trudged along the trail as it meandered between tufts of dry grass growing as high as her thighs. Thank goodness the fire was under control. It would have raced across this area, engulfing the brittle grass. She picked her way down a set of stone stairs, catching glimpses of turquoise and cobalt water in rocky coves. A final curve of the trail revealed a petite beach, and she felt her shoulders sag with relief. She'd been worried she'd taken a wrong turn, since a few other trails had branched out from the main one.

A narrow inlet of water, edged on both sides with sloping rock walls, shimmered, the water transitioning from pale aqua shades at the shore to swaths of azure as the water deepened. The color shifted again to a sapphire blue where the inlet met the sea. The beach was deserted, but once she descended the steps, she saw evidence of former visitors, a discarded orange peel and a couple of caps from San Pellegrino bottles. Instead of sand, the beach was a rock beach with smooth stones, some of them as large as her fist, covering the whole shore stretching from the water back to the edge of the cliff that enclosed the inlet. There were several huge rocks, a few taller than Zoe, at the back of the beach. She settled her back against one of them and put the paintings at her side. The rocks were dry, and there was no chance of water coming up this high onto the beach.

Water lapped on the rocky beach, the sun inched lower, and Zoe tried to ignore the gnawing feeling in her stomach. Her sprint, not to mention the hike to the beach, had burned off her large lunch at the café, but she really wanted water more than she wanted food. However, there was nothing but the salty water slapping against the rocks.

The smooth rocks were surprisingly comfortable. Her thoughts weren't. What if Jack didn't show up? What would she do? She'd left her messenger bag in the car when they followed Anna to the villa so she had no passport or money.

But she did have a stolen Monet painting.

She didn't even want to think about how she'd ever explain what had happened. And she didn't want to think about Jack not showing up. She'd have to go back to the village. With the paintings.

Don't go there. It hasn't happened yet. Deal with it later, if you have to.

She stretched out fully on the rocks and stared at the cloudless sky.

No water, no food, no money, no identification. And she'd just shoved away the one person who knew the whole situation and had been willing to help her, no questions asked.

That thought pattern wouldn't do her any good. She crossed her hands on her stomach and tried to clear her mind. Maybe she could drift into a nap. She should be exhausted, but after about three minutes, she sat up. It was hard to get comfortable with the tender spot on the back of her skull.

She pulled off her shoes, rolled up her jeans, and went to the water. It spilled over her pale feet, shockingly cold, and drenched her ankles. Zoe gasped and jumped back. Who knew the Mediterranean was so frigid in March?

She stayed back where only the frothy edges of the waves swirled around her feet as she walked. No matter how hard she tried to avoid them, the thoughts wouldn't go away.

She'd been so sure of herself when she and Jack argued, but now a curl of doubt spiraled in her. Was he right? Did she hold everyone off, even Helen, not letting anyone get too close?

Marrying Jack had been an anomaly. Everyone who knew her had been shocked that she'd married, but even then, she hadn't gone all in. She'd held back. Jack had, too, keeping his secrets. No wonder their marriage had disintegrated into cold silences on Jack's part and heated words on hers.

She thought back to the almost argument she'd had with

Helen in the bookstore where she'd listed her reasons` for not getting back together with Jack. He'd lied to her, deceived her. They were great together when they were under pressure and in extreme circumstances, but it didn't work in real life. What if she was wrong? What if now that there were no lies or deception between them, what if they were really good—maybe even great—in normal life? Were her reasons for not getting together with Jack just an excuse, a smoke screen, to keep him from getting too close?

She watched the chilly water foam around her ankles as she thought about her friends. She was closer to Helen than anyone, but most of her friends were surface friends, like Carla. She knew them, kept in touch, went to lunch or went for a run, but there was no real depth to the relationship.

She reached the end of the beach and splashed back the other way. Was she a fraud? Instead of being a fearless nonconformist, was she really just a distrustful skeptic? In the parts of life that really counted—friends and family—was she playing it close to the vest, holding back instead of plunging in with both feet as she did in everything else? She kicked through the water with a stronger stride, flinging a spray of droplets over her clothes.

Her thoughts circled back to her other worry. *What if Jack doesn't show?* What would she do? She'd basically told him they were over. Why would he come? Why put himself at risk?

She came to a standstill. A wave washed up, soaking a few inches of her jeans. Was steady, reliable, keep-his-head-down-and-get-the-job-done Jack a bigger risk-taker than she was?

HOURS later, Zoe was seriously considering gnawing on the orange peel she'd seen earlier. The problem was she doubted she'd be able to find it. It was completely dark now. It could be any time between seven and midnight. Unlike Jack, who had a watch that did everything but function as a GPS, her watch was only a watch. Not even glow-in-the-dark numbers or hands. The sun had dropped below the horizon a little after six, and by six-thirty, the thick blackness engulfed her. As the minutes stretched, she tested the saying about not being able to see your hand in front of your face and found she could see it. Just barely. She could make out dim shapes of the larger rocks. A thin strip of moon didn't give any significant light, and the specks of starlight reflecting on the water gave off only pinpricks of light.

Zoe was a city girl and found the intensity of the darkness unnerving. The scuttling sounds along the rocks hadn't bothered her in the daylight—lizards, she'd assumed. But now in the near blackness, she jumped every time she heard a scurrying sound. Lizards. They had to be lizards, she told herself. She wouldn't let herself think of any other options.

A black mass shifted in the water. Zoe held herself still as whatever it was moved on a steady course, darkening the speckles of light on the water, straight to the beach. Something scraped against rock, louder than the low splash of the lapping tide. Zoe hoped the dots on her shirt blended with the light-colored rocks enough that it didn't stand out in the dimness.

A narrow beam of light clicked on and swept across the rocks. "Zoe?"

Relief washed over her. "Here. I'm over here," she called softly, matching Jack's low tone. In that moment, she realized just how afraid she had been that he wouldn't show up.

The beam of light danced across the rocks to her. She threw up a hand. "Shut that thing off, would you?"

"Well, that's a fine way to greet your rescuer." The light went off.

Zoe could hear the smile in his voice. "I am glad to see you, believe me. You have no idea how glad, but I can't see a thing with that light on."

"It's better we leave it off anyway. Want some water?"

"You brought water?" Trust Jack to not only come to her rescue, but to bring water, too. "You really are the best." She waved her hand around until it connected with his extended arm. She took the bottle and chugged. "Jack, about earlier today..."

She heard a gusty sigh. "Let's not do this now, okay? Let's get out of here, get this mess straightened out, then we can go our separate ways."

His exact, arm's-length tone pierced her. But it was what she wanted—him to back off. She swallowed, suddenly thankful for the darkness. He was right. They had bigger things to worry about than their relationship. "Right. Okay." She patted the rocks until she touched the canvases. She tried to match his all-business tone, but didn't quite succeed. "I found the Monet. The real one."

"I didn't doubt you would for a minute."

"Liar," she said lightly.

"Well, maybe for one minute, but that's all," Jack said, and Zoe felt them slipping back into the 'everything's fine' mode that they'd operated on many times before their divorce. Light banter on the surface covering deep cracks in their relationship. "In fact," Jack continued, "I brought something to wrap it." A crackle of plastic sounded. "I'm going to put the light on for a second. Over this way?"

"Yes."

Zoe turned her head away as the light burst on, but Jack shielded it with his hand, so it wasn't nearly as bright as before. Against the gray and white of the rocks, the colors of the painting popped, bright and vibrant. He let out a low whistle. "Well done."

"Thanks. There's more." She angled the first one back and showed him the second painting. "One of Giorgio's copies, so we can prove what they were doing."

"Even better. One small detail, how do you know which is which?"

"The back. Remember what Masard said about the markings? Well, this painting has stickers and stamps. The copy is as pristine as a field of new snow."

"Excellent."

"So glad you brought something to put them in." Zoe shook out the large plastic shopping bag. "I was worried about damaging it...the sun and dust, not to mention my sweaty hands." Jack transferred the flashlight to his mouth and helped her slip both paintings inside. They fit with only an inch to spare.

"Where did you get the bag?"

"Remember our friends at the café?"

"Isobel and...Paul, wasn't it?"

"Yes. Isobel had done some shopping by the time I caught up with them a few hours ago. She let me borrow it, along with a few other things."

Zoe folded the edges of the plastic over and picked up the now empty water bottle. "Okay. Let's get out of here."

Jack switched off the light. "This way." He caught her free hand and guided her to the water. Zoe had expected a boat-shaped object, something narrow and long, but as her hand traced along the side of the craft, she realized it was square. "What is this?"

Jack didn't say a word, just clicked on the light, again sheltering it with his hand.

Zoe blinked. "That's a paddleboat."

"Afraid so."

"Okay."

"Best I could do on short notice. The good news is we only have to use it to get to the boat that's waiting for us outside this inlet. This is a nature preserve, so no boats are allowed in here, not that Aldo could get his boat this close, anyway. Too shallow. Shall we?" Jack extended his hand.

Zoe gripped it and stepped into the paddleboat, carefully settling the paintings on her lap. Jack shoved the paddleboat into the water as he splashed around to his side. They put their feet on the pedals and had a few false starts as they reversed and turned, but they got the hang of it, and the little boat glided across the inky water. "This is really amazing," Zoe said, looking up at the sky. With the starlight above her and the gentle waves swishing alongside the boat, catching fragments of light, she felt like she was in a kaleidoscope.

Jack agreed then said, "On a more mundane note, are you hungry?"

"Starving."

"I thought you might be." As he pedaled, Jack reached around behind his seat. "I got some bars. Not sure what kind they are—nut and fruit, I think. My Italian is getting rusty. There are a few bananas, too."

Zoe handed one bar to Jack, then ripped one open for herself and ate it in three bites. "Almond and cranberry." She peeled the banana. "Thanks."

"Sure. I need all the help with the pedaling I can get."

"My thighs hurt already, and I've only been doing this a few minutes." She tucked the banana peel and the wrappers back in the small bag and removed another bottle of water. "So, the fire. What happened?"

"Anna's cigarette touched it off. They had it under control quickly. Probably less than an hour. Very impressive, actually. They take their forest fire fighting seriously around here, I guess. I didn't stick around. Once I saw you turn and head for the beach and saw that Anna and Giorgio were clear of the fire, I headed back to the village. The fire brigade—or whatever they're called here—was already moving in. I was lucky to get out of there before they shut down the road."

"So you went back to Positano?"

"Yeah. I figured I could get a boat there to come get you. There's no other way to get to that beach."

"So how did you convince Aldo to bring his boat out to get me at...what...midnight?"

"The night is still young. At least, in some bars in Positano, it is. I found an ATM and used my credit card to get a cash advance. I used part of the money to hire Aldo. When he saw I had cash, he didn't have a problem with going out late, or bringing the paddleboat."

They were nearing the point where the inlet met the sea and the paddleboat was now riding larger waves up to their crest then dipping into the troughs. Zoe gripped the plastic around the edge of the painting and pedaled harder as they surged with the waves. The paddleboat felt miniscule in the rolling sea. Around the headland of rocks that enclosed the bay, a white hull of a motorboat loomed.

They pedaled to a deck at the back where a man waited for them, his hand outstretched to help them aboard. It wasn't a large boat, but compared to the paddleboat, it felt spacious. With the paintings hugged to her chest, Zoe dropped onto one of the motorboat's vinyl seats. She could see an outline of another small boat, this one with inflatable sides and an outboard motor, bobbing in the water beside them. Once Jack was aboard, the captain of their boat attached the paddleboat to the inflatable boat. A shadowy figure in the other boat helped him secure the paddleboat, then they exchanged a few words in Italian, and the captain of the inflatable started the engine and putted slowly away, towing the paddleboat.

"That's Aldo's son," Jack said, lifting his chin in the direction of the disappearing boat. "He rents the paddleboat out during the day to tourists who want to explore the beaches and a little grotto not far from here."

Their captain went forward and started the boat. By the light of the control panel Zoe could see he was completely bald, but had a neat black beard. A red bandana circled his throat above a loose white shirt and dark pants. The boat surged, the bow rising as he pushed the throttle forward. Zoe clasped the paintings, as the plastic around them flapped in the sudden breeze with one hand and held her hat firmly with the other. The captain shouted something over his shoulder to Jack, his bandana and shirt pulsing against his body in the wind.

"What did he say?"

"We'll be there in a few minutes."

"Where?"

"The *Regent Renaissance*."

18

They skimmed across the water toward Capri. Lights from the town ringed the semi-circle of the harbor and sprinkled up the hillside that cupped the inlet, but Zoe's gaze was on the cruise ship that was anchored outside the harbor. "How did you manage to get us on the cruise ship?" she asked. "That must have cost a boatload."

"I suppose I could have tried to bribe someone, but a trade seemed easier. Nice pun, by the way."

"Couldn't help it. What kind of trade?"

Jack handed Zoe a lanyard with an ID card. She flipped it over and saw Isobel's picture and name.

Jack draped another lanyard with a dangling card over his neck. "I gave our rental car to Isobel and Paul."

"What?"

"It's perfectly logical. They don't want to go back on the ship and we do. I went back to the hotel they'd asked us about. They'd checked in and were in the bar, so I explained that it was urgent you speak to your friend on the ship, that it was a rather delicate situation. You needed to see him face-to-face. They agreed to a swap. They're meeting us at the Rome airport in two days. I told them we'd pack their belongings and bring them with us. In the meantime, while we're on board, they'll visit Pompeii."

"I can't believe you gave them the car. They could wreck it...or...I don't know...steal it."

Jack lowered his chin and gave her a long look. "Zoe, he's a pharmacist, and she's a history teacher. I don't think they'll go Grand Theft Auto on us. Besides, we have bigger things to worry about." His gaze slid to the plastic-wrapped paintings in Zoe's lap.

"That's true. This is worth more rental cars than I can even figure up in my head."

Jack nodded toward the towering cruise ship. "Okay. Here we go, Mrs...." he paused to check his lanyard, "Johnston. Keep that hat on, and we'll sail through."

"Hmm, I can see we may need a moratorium on the boating puns, Mr. Johnston."

The motorboat had felt roomy after the paddleboat, but when they pulled along the cruise ship, Zoe felt as if their boat was a minnow swimming next to a whale.

The captain shouted to Jack over his shoulder.

"He says that the harbor isn't deep enough here for the big ships. They anchor out here and boats ferry people to and from." Jack reached for another plastic shopping bag that Zoe hadn't noticed and opened it. "Clothes. I thought bringing a suitcase on board at this point in the cruise might look a tad suspicious." Zoe's messenger bag had been under the bag of clothes.

"How are we going to find Mort?" Zoe asked as she slipped her messenger bag over her shoulder.

"That's your department. I got us here. You've got a plan, right?"

"Umm...no. Not off the top of my head. I've been thinking about the painting mostly. Is it too much to hope that Kathy will post a convenient status update about being on the Lido Deck or something? It's a long shot, but it's the only thing I can think of right now. There's got to be a way to page someone, or get them a message."

"Let's get on the ship, first, then see what we can find out. It's only ten. He and Kathy might still be up."

"Ten? That can't be right. I thought it was after midnight." Jack hit the button to illuminate his watch and tilted it toward her. "That means I was only on that beach for a few hours. It felt like...I don't know...about eight. I guess time drags when you're *not* having fun."

The captain of their now miniscule-feeling ship maneuvered close to a canopy-covered staircase that dropped down from a door in the ship's hull to the water level. Embracing the painting, Zoe climbed out of the boat and up the staircase.

"I can see why Isobel wouldn't want to come back here."

After an uninterested cruise ship employee watched them scan their cards at the top of the stairs then ran their bags through a scanner, it had taken them thirty minutes to find Isobel and Paul's room. "Just keep moving," Jack had said. "Act like you know where you're going."

Which was hard to pull off when you had no clue about the layout of the ship, but after unintentionally touring the ship's huge central shopping atrium and three different sets of staircases that took them the wrong way, they'd finally stumbled on Isobel and Paul's room in the bowels of the ship.

Zoe stepped into the windowless room. "I think it's actually smaller than our rooms in Paris." A gap of a few inches separated the double bed from the walls. Towels folded into the shape of an elephant rested on the bed. There was a closet on one side of the bed, a narrow desk attached to the wall, and a door to a tiny bathroom on the other.

Jack closed the door. "You're exaggerating." Zoe had to step out of the way and squish down the narrow opening between the bed and the closet so that Jack could enter the room and close the door.

"Not much." She pushed open one of the sliding closet doors.

"I think this is the only place big enough to hide the paintings.

"Would you like to go first?" Jack asked, waving to the bathroom.

"Yes. I feel positively gritty."

"All right. I'll take care of the paintings."

They'd decided it wasn't wise to tote the paintings around while they tried to locate Mort. Their game plan was to locate their temporary cabin, stash the paintings, and clean up because they were both kind of scruffy. Zoe's rumpled, dusty shirt and jeans had drawn a few curious stares as they traipsed the passageways and staircases looking for the cabin. Most people were dressed up, with many of the women in cocktail dresses and the men in suits.

The shower was tiny and she bumped her elbows on the walls more times than she could count, but she didn't care. It felt heavenly to get clean. She wielded the blow dryer until her hair was mostly dry, then slipped on the only dress she'd packed, the emerald green wrap dress with cap sleeves. It wasn't as dressy as the clothes she'd seen earlier as they searched for the cabin, but it was all she had.

"Do you think I'll do? Will I blend? It's not very dressy..." Zoe broke off when she saw Jack's face.

"You'll more than do."

Zoe swallowed and tried to fight off the blush she felt seeping into her face and neck. "Thanks. Your turn." They sidled by each other. The room was so tight it was impossible not to brush against each other.

As soon as he shut the bathroom door, Zoe turned to the mirror mounted on the wall above a set of recessed drawers. She put her hands on her rosy cheeks. They could not stay in these close quarters long. She couldn't deny the attraction between them. Rekindling things with Jack wasn't what she wanted she told herself firmly, but a faint question wormed its way into her thoughts. Was it? Was that really what she wanted? "Not a good idea," she lectured herself.

The bathroom door opened. "Did you say something?" Jack leaned out the door, his shirt unbuttoned.

With great effort, Zoe pulled her gaze away from that strip of taut, tan chest and cleared her throat. "No. Nothing. Nothing at all."

He closed the bathroom door, and she stared at her flushed face as his words came back to her. *You're afraid.* Was he right? Did she push him away and fight to keep their relationship from going deeper because she was scared? But what was there to be scared of? Intimacy? A close, loving relationship? Jack had made it clear he wanted more than a fling. What would it be like to let herself trust him?

The sound of the shower coming on brought her out of her reverie. She yanked open the zipper on her makeup bag and set to work with mascara and lip-gloss. Now was not the time to figure out her love life.

It only took her a few minutes to finish her make-up then she checked the paintings. Jack had tucked them along the back wall of the closet behind Isobel and Paul's suitcases and adjusted the clothes on hangers so that not even an inch of the plastic bag showed. The paintings were well hidden from anyone who gave the room or the closet a casual glance. While she was in the closet, she spotted a pair of gold open-toe, sling-back stilettos. She couldn't resist slipping them on, and they were a perfect fit. She didn't think Isobel would mind if she borrowed them. After all, Isobel was borrowing their rental car. What was a pair of shoes compared to a car?

She was trying to maneuver into a spot in front of the mirror where she could see how the shoes looked with the dress when a knock on the cabin door sounded. Zoe froze, one foot extended in the air in front of the mirror.

The rapping came again, louder this time. "Mr. Johnston, it is Raoul. I have your tea."

Zoe inched to the door and spoke to the doorframe. "Thank you, but we didn't order tea."

"But Mr. Johnston always has tea in the evening. To settle his stomach."

"He's feeling better tonight and doesn't need it." Zoe bit her lip. They were busted. This had to be the cabin steward. He knew Isobel and Paul, and he wasn't going away.

"Are you not feeling well either, Mrs. Johnston? You sound funny."

Zoe blew out a breath and opened the door. "I'm not Mrs. Johnston."

Raoul paused on the threshold, a tray held aloft. "We're friends of Isobel and Paul. We've traded with them." Her conscious pricked her as she remembered Jack's words about lying by omission.

"Oh, you can't do that." Raoul looked to be in his early twenties with golden hair combed back from an angular face that if it wasn't scowling, would have been very attractive.

She squashed down her misgivings. It was for a good cause—to keep her out of jail, and her friends and family from harm. She straightened her shoulders and smiled brightly. "A little joke."

Raoul's gaze dipped for an instant to the *V* of her neckline, and there was a flash of a question in his dark eyes.

"Come in, and I'll tell you about it," Zoe said in as flirty a tone as she could manage. She wasn't used to playing the femme fatale, and wondered if she was overdoing it, but he stepped inside.

Zoe closed the door and reached for her messenger bag as he set the tray down. She removed several bills from her wallet and held them out. What was the going rate for a bribe? She had no idea, but decided it would be better to go high rather than low. He raised his hand to wave Zoe off, but then he saw the denomination of the notes in the little wad of cash. "You'll help me keep my secret, won't you?" Zoe asked.

He sent her a smile and plucked the bills from her hand. "My job is to make sure you are happy. Will there be anything else?" His look and his tone indicated that there was very little he wouldn't be willing to do.

"Just one other small thing."

JACK emerged from the bath wearing a pair of dark pants

and a white dress shirt with a striped tie draped across his shoulders. He caught sight of the tray as he knotted his tie.

"Apparently, Paul has a cup of tea every evening to calm his stomach. I had to take the cabin steward into our confidence."

Jack paused with his chin raised and his fingers stilled. "Was that wise?"

"We didn't have a choice. He knows Isobel and Paul. He recognized my voice wasn't Isobel's, and if he gave us away, then the game would be up. So I convinced him to keep our secret. I said we were playing a joke."

"And he agreed?" Jack worked the knot into place.

"With a little help from my cleavage and a wad of euros, yes."

Jack's eyes narrowed.

"You were the one who mentioned bribery."

"No. You brought that up, and I would never involve you or...your cleavage..."

A faint knock cut off Jack's sputtering. A white envelope slipped under the door.

Zoe snatched it up and read the paper inside. "He was able to do it! Mort used his drink card at the Mariner Bar ten minutes ago."

Jack raised his eyebrows.

"I asked Raoul if there was a way to find someone on the ship. He said he would check. They can track the pre-paid drink card."

"Well, I am glad Raoul is so helpful. Do you think he'll give us away, now that your cleavage isn't on display?"

"No, because I told him there would be more for him in the morning, if he kept quiet."

"More what?" Jack said in an unpleasant tone.

"Money," Zoe said impatiently. "Forget about my cleavage. That's not what's important here. We know where Mort is. We need to get moving."

Jack's scowl disappeared and his face went blank. "You're correct. I have no right to be jealous. Let's go. He might not stay there long."

Jack swiped his lanyard, which was also the room's keycard, off the narrow dresser and went out the door. "That's not what I meant," Zoe muttered as she looked at the ceiling. Relationships were a minefield. It was a wonder that anyone ever got together at all, she thought as she hurried out the door.

BY the time Zoe caught up with Jack, he'd found the Mariner Bar, a larger space fitted with dark paneling, brass lights, and potted ferns. Her conflicted feeling about their relationship —or lack thereof—had to take a backseat. "I don't see Mort," Zoe said, scanning the room, which was crowded with people in fancy dress, some around the bar, others gathered around the cushy armchairs and tiny tables, while still others danced at one end of the room where a guy was belting out *The Way You Look Tonight* in front of a small band.

"It's crowded. He might still be here. Let's get a drink."

Zoe reluctantly followed Jack to the bar, fighting down the urge to search the passageways outside the bar. Jack offered Zoe the single open barstool. "Gin and tonic?"

"Club soda with a twist of lime. I don't want to get fuzzy."

Zoe thought she heard Jack murmur, "Well I need one." She gave him a sharp look, but he didn't glance at her, only tossed back a swig of his drink. She sipped hers, alternating between watching the door and looking at each face in the room.

A smattering of applause sounded as the song ended. Jack touched her arm. "There." He pointed with his glass. As the couples on the dance floor broke apart and some left, Zoe spotted a rumpled figure with a thatch of unruly gray hair. She'd never met Mort's wife, Kathy, but the woman with the fluffy blond hair stepping into his outstretched arms for the next dance had to be her. Jack finished his drink and held out his hand. "Shall we?"

She put her hand in his. "Now I wish I'd had a real drink."

They made for the dance floor. Mort was at the far side, and Zoe was about to push her way through the couples when Jack swung her around into his arms. "We'll work our way over there. Don't want to draw too much attention. We are stowaways."

"Right. I forgot for a moment." They moved to the music, *Fly Me To The Moon*, Jack smoothly navigating them through the other couples, a good five inches separating their bodies. "You know, I don't think we've ever danced before," Zoe said. She had to say something to block out the sudden thoughts about how he smelled like soap and how his shoulder flexed under her hand as they moved. It felt so good in his arms, so right, which was an absurd thought since his rigid posture and shuttered expression showed he clearly wasn't enjoying being close to her.

He moved his hand on the small of her back, pulling her closer as he swung her away from a tipsy couple plowing across the dance floor. He swirled them around a few times, and Zoe felt as though she'd had a drink or two by the time he slowed down. "And here we are." Jack released her, tapped

Mort on the shoulder, and offered his hand to Kathy. “May I cut in?”

Kathy looked slightly surprised, but sent Mort a wink as she reached for Jack’s hand. “Can’t pass this up.”

“Why do I think my vacation just ended?” Mort said.

19

"You can tell this one is the real one because of the back." Zoe carefully lifted the canvas to show Mort the marks on the back.

Earlier, at a table in the back of the bar, she had recapped everything that had happened since she entered Lucinda's backyard. Mort let her get through the whole thing and only asked one question. "The paintings are on this ship?"

"Yes, in our cabin."

"We better start there."

Jack and Kathy had come with them, and now the four of them were crowded into the small cabin, leaning over the end of the bed where Zoe had put the two paintings side-by-side.

She moved to the other canvas. "This one, the forgery, is blank. That's how the dealer in Paris said he knew the one Anna brought him was a fake. Well, it was the main reason. There were other indications. He talked about brush strokes and the signature, too, but the back was the biggest factor."

Half glasses perched on his nose, Mort examined the two paintings with Kathy hanging over his shoulder.

"A real Monet," she sighed. "I can't believe I'm this close to one. The two paintings are similar, but there's something about this one..." Kathy indicated the one with the markings on the back. "I don't know how to describe it. It has an extra *something* that makes it...I don't know...sing."

Zoe tilted her head, studying the two paintings. Now that they were isolated away from the mass of similar paintings at the villa and placed next to each other, there was a difference. "I see it, too. It's like it has more...oomph."

"It has an effervescence," Kathy said, and Mort looked over his glasses at her. She shrugged. "It does. Don't you see it?"

"I'm more concerned with getting it into a safe."

"Spoil sport," Kathy said, but then she grinned. "Once a cop, always a cop."

Mort removed his glasses. "Looks like I'm going to have to turn on my cell phone. Almost made it two whole weeks without doing that." Kathy volunteered to return to their cabin to get the cell phone while Jack replaced the paintings in the plastic bag.

"Sorry to ruin your vacation," Zoe said.

He glanced at the door Kathy had just left through. "Bridge had begun to lose its allure. But you didn't hear it from me." He picked up several pieces of cruise ship stationary. "Now, let's go through this again, make sure I have everything clear." He sat down at the narrow desk while Zoe perched on the edge of the bed. Mort resettled his glasses on his nose and made notes as he asked, "So when are you supposed to contact this Oscar, now that you have the painting that Mr. Gray wants?"

"He gave us a deadline of tomorrow."

"And how are you supposed to do that?"

Zoe handed him the business card from her messenger bag. He centered it up on the desk in front of him. Mort scribbled away in silence for a few moments. Jack moved to the bathroom and leaned against the doorframe.

"You see, we thought that if we called the local police, it would be, well, a nightmare. It is a stolen Monet, after all. And we knew leaving the country with it wouldn't be smart."

"You could have called the FBI office in Dallas."

Zoe pressed her lips together. No use beating around the bush. "I wasn't sure they'd hear me out, and with Lucinda..." Zoe swallowed and forced herself to go on, "With her body in my backyard."

Mort looked up from the paper and nodded. "I can see that."

"But we didn't want to give it back to Mr. Gray either. You know him?"

"I recognize the name, yes. He's been on the Bureau's radar for a long time."

"So you know what kind of guy he is." Zoe looked at the plastic bag covering the paintings. "First of all, it's a masterpiece. If Mr. Gray gets that painting, he'll sell it or stash it in that free port place Oscar mentioned. It might not be found for years, if ever. I know that's the least important factor here. It is only a painting, even if it is a masterpiece. But that was part of it. Then there was Lucinda. If we gave the painting back, then Gray would get away with murder. And finally, if we gave it back, Mr. Gray might go back on his word. He said he'd take care of Lucinda's body, and I wouldn't be blamed, but once he had the painting—"

"He would have no reason to care what happened to you."

"Yes," Zoe said.

"No good choice, anyway you look at it."

Zoe licked her lips. "So, we thought the only thing to do was offer it to the FBI."

"Through me? I'm retired."

"But you have connections. You still know people. And you knew our background, everything that had happened with the fraud case." Mort gave a reluctant nod, and Zoe continued, "We'll turn the Monet over to the FBI, and give them all the information we have about Mr. Gray. They can use it to catch him."

"Aren't you forgetting something? Don't you want immunity in exchange for the painting and your testimony?"

"But we don't need immunity. We didn't kill Lucinda or steal the Monet...oh, I see what you mean. We did steal it from Anna. But she'd stolen it, too."

Jack spoke up. "Add immunity to our list."

"Wise choice." Mort ran his hand over his mouth as he looked at the paper. "Okay. So you're thinking the FBI will take possession of the painting and set up a sting to catch Mr. Gray—all before tomorrow? On foreign soil?"

Zoe and Jack exchanged a glance.

"Are you saying they couldn't do it? Or, that they wouldn't be interested?"

"No. They'll be interested. We better get to work. Why don't you order us some coffee? It's going to be a long night."

AFTER the painting was secured in the largest safety deposit box on the ship, and Zoe had added the key to the long chain that hung heavy on her neck with her wedding ring, they had moved to Mort and Kathy's cabin, which was bigger and had a balcony.

Mort hunched over the desk and made several long phone calls, while Zoe and Jack sat on the balcony with Kathy, who brought her knitting with her and added several inches to a scarf while they waited. It was a pleasant evening, cool, but not cold, and they chatted intermittently, talking about Italy and the ports Kathy and Mort had visited on the cruise, but it was a strained conversation. They were all listening to the low mumble from the cabin through the balcony's open sliding glass door.

Zoe assumed Mort was talking to his old colleagues in Dallas. It was close to six in the evening there, and she wondered how hard it would be for Mort to get in contact with the people he needed to talk to. With the difference in time zones, it would be at least three o'clock in the afternoon tomorrow in Italy before the workday started in Dallas. They couldn't wait that long.

After the fourth call, Mort turned to the balcony. "Sato is in the air, on his way here."

"To Italy?" Zoe asked incredulously.

"Yes. He lands in Rome at seven tomorrow morning." Mort crossed the room and stood in the doorway to the balcony. "He got the information about the financial transactions—the ones you said Darius Gray mentioned—but Sato's new partner thought something looked off. The analyst took another look and discovered the transactions were an elaborate red herring, set up to frame you," Mort said, looking at Zoe.

She closed her eyes for a moment. "Do they know about Lucinda?"

"She's officially missing now. She's not on the manifest of any airline that flew out of Dallas in the last week."

"So they haven't found her body?"

"No. There's a team on their way to your house now to search the backyard."

Zoe nodded, her glance slipping to Jack, as she said, "No going back now."

Who was she kidding? Once she'd told Mort everything, their course had been set. They'd thrown their lots in on the side of the good guys. She just hoped it was the right choice.

Jack said, "It's good that they discovered the financial transactions were falsified. Once they find Lucinda's body, it will confirm your story."

"I know, but somehow I don't find it very comforting that a dead body is my proof. That's just not good." She stood and walked to the edge of the balcony where she leaned against the rail.

Mort cleared his throat and said, "The Italian police will meet Sato at the airport, bring him here. The original plan was for him to go to Naples, your last location that he knew of, but I've left messages for him to come here, to Capri."

"What agency are the officials from? The ones who are bringing him?" Jack asked. "I only ask because I had some rather unpleasant experiences with the Italian police."

"I understand your skittishness. You did have some encounters with people who should not be allowed to wear a law enforcement uniform, but you don't have anything to worry about here. Interpol is involved and has sent a representative as well as the Italian Art Theft Squad."

"They know about the painting?" Zoe asked, her hand tight on the railing.

"A payment for an invoice listing an Impressionist painting was the only transaction on the account of Verity Trustees. Once Sato contacted the Bureau's art squad, they immediately got in touch with their Italian counterparts, who take art theft very seriously." There was a knock at the door. "Ah, that should be my summons to the captain. I must explain why I am harboring two stowaways and arrange transportation to Capri for us. You might want to change. I think it will take some time at the police station."

THE clash of voices woke her. She squinted against the bright florescent lights. She was in a Capri police station. She had a crick in her neck and her arm was asleep, but the upside was that she wasn't locked in a cell.

Last night, after she'd thrown on the last of her clean clothes, a pair of white capri pants with a navy and white striped shirt, she, Jack, and Mort had boarded a motorboat under the disapproving eye of the cruise ship's captain.

They left the paintings in the safety deposit box, which made Zoe nervous, although she knew it shouldn't. "Until everything is agreed, it is best that they are in a secure, unknown place," Mort had said.

Two Carabinieri officers, looking sharp in their dark uniforms with the red stripe down the leg, had greeted them as if it was perfectly normal to meet people at Capri's *Marina Grande* at two o'clock in the morning. The officers, part of the Italian national military police force, drove them up a road that switched back on itself as it climbed up from the harbor between white stone walls. They stopped at a plain, oblong building perched on the hillside between the harbor and the sheer white limestone cliffs.

They were treated as guests, offered drinks, and questioned together. Zoe had a feeling this was in deference to Mort, a fellow law officer, even if he was retired. Jack's ability to translate the essentials of their situation helped as well. In a conference room with a view of the harbor, she'd told her story to a revolving cast of officers, who all seemed to have different uniforms and different questions and concerns. "How many different police forces do they have here?" Zoe had hissed to Jack after their fourth round. Even the tax police had taken their turn.

"It's Italy," Jack had said with a shrug. "Of course, it is convoluted."

Eventually, the questions tapered off and written agreements between her and Jack and the various police agencies were drawn up, spelling out that Zoe and Jack would receive immunity in exchange for the painting and their testimony against Gray.

When the last stack of paper was signed, their first Carabinieri interviewer returned, Lieutenant Colonel Russo, a fortyish man with a serious face, steady dark brown eyes, and a sweep of gray in his dark hair at his temples. Russo spoke some English. "Now we wait for the arrival of your colleague from the United States." Since there was nothing else to do, Zoe paced the room for a while, but she couldn't stay on her feet long. She had stretched out on a couch at the back of the room and drifted in and out of sleep.

She shifted and sat up, pins and needles stinging her arm as she moved. Jack was in one of the conference chairs, his eyes closed and his feet propped up in another chair. Beyond him, on the other side of the room, Sato and Mort stood with a new group of people, all talking and gesturing.

Jack opened one eye at the sound of her movement.

She dipped her head toward the far end of the room. "Sato's here and—wait—it's not a trick of the light. His shirt is actually wrinkled." Every time Zoe had seen Sato he was perfectly turned out in immaculate designer suits. But now his tie was loose, and he'd removed his suit coat and rolled up his sleeves. "This is serious."

Jack dropped his feet to the floor as he scrubbed his face as the voices grew louder and arms flung wider to emphasize points. "Is it just me, or do things seem to be getting out of control?" Zoe asked in an undertone as she rotated her head, trying to work the kink out of her neck.

Jack listened, then said, "They're debating the best way to take Gray down. They all have a different idea on how to do it."

"Isn't that a little premature? We don't even know where he is...or if he'll be there to pick up the painting himself."

"He's gone to a lot of trouble to get the painting," Jack said. "He might want to see it right away."

"Or, he might send someone to get it for him, like Oscar."

"They'll trail the courier and hope he—or she—leads them back to Gray."

"But Gray could send an anonymous person to pick it up and take it straight to one of those free port places." Zoe shook out her arm and noticed the time. "It's ten," she said, looking at Jack with wide eyes, then to the window where late morning sunlight slanted over the mix of rocks, trees, and houses that rose up from the vibrant blue of the water. "I have to call him soon."

Sato, who had been in conversation with the dark-haired Carabinieri official, moved to Zoe and Jack. "It's time to make the call."

20

Zoe stared at the business card on the table, her cell phone gripped in her hand, trying to look like she was a normal tourist, enjoying coffee at a harbor-side café.

Jack sat on her right. Sato was at the next table, his gaze focused on his watch. Dark circles shadowed his eyes. She was sure she didn't look much better after getting only a few hours of sleep on the couch, but the difference was that she didn't specialize in sartorial splendor while it was Sato's hallmark. She and Jack had arrived separately from Sato, and she was doing her best not to let her gaze slip toward him too often. Without looking up, Sato said, "I heard you weren't anxious to contact me." He spoke so softly that only Zoe and Jack could hear him.

Zoe put the phone down and wiped her palms against her pant leg. "If you were me, would you want to call the FBI office with my story?" she asked under her breath.

One side of his mouth turned up. "Point taken." His smile vanished. "Okay. They're ready. You can make the call."

Zoe blew out a breath and dialed the number. In case

Gray had a way to track where the cell originated from, they'd moved from the police station to the café. She'd caught a glimpse of two regular police officers strolling the street as well as the tax police. She was sure there were other police officers around that she couldn't see.

The phone rang several times. She darted a look at Jack. Was she going to have to leave a message on voicemail? They'd gone over so many details about the call before they left the police station. She wore a wire threaded through the collar of her shirt that she'd been told was so sensitive that it would be able to pick up the voice on the other end of the call. She had rehearsed what to say, practicing phrases that would give the police as much time as possible to fine tune the plans before the hand-off of the painting.

The one thing she hadn't prepared for was leaving a message. She had the urge to laugh and knew it was a reaction to the tension. What was she going to say? *Your painting is ready for pick-up.* Or, *got the Monet. Call me.* She squelched the giddiness and put on her serious face. Under the table, Sato made a sharp cutting motion with his hand. She ended the call before the recorded message came on.

She dropped the phone on the table and put her head in her hands, her elbows on the table. "He's not going to answer. He's figured out we've gone to the police," she whispered.

Thoughts swirled through her mind sucking the momentary hilarity away and replacing it with panic. The agreements they'd made with the police...would they still be valid if Gray disappeared? If Gray wasn't caught, they couldn't testify. Would the police go back on the agreements? And what about the painting? Now they only had Zoe and Jack's word that Gray had forced them to go after it.

A tightness squeezed down on her chest. *Was it all going to fall apart?*

The phone buzzed, and Zoe jerked away from it as it vibrated. It was a text that read, "Dock 5. 1 p.m. Come alone. Bring the item."

She realized that she'd read it aloud. As Sato stood, he murmured, "Wait until I'm gone, then pick up the painting and go to the restaurant as planned."

Jack signaled for their check and paid for the coffees they'd barely touched. It was only a few steps to the dock where Mort waited, already seated on a boat that would take them back to the cruise ship. They still had their lanyards and showed them to the cruise ship attendant who stood at the gangplank. He waved them onto the boat, and as they'd agreed earlier, Zoe and Jack slipped by Mort, who was seated at the midpoint of the boat, without a word and moved to the back of the boat. This was the cruise ship's tender, the small boat used to ferry passengers to and from port, so they had to wait a few minutes as a few other cruise ship passengers boarded. Once they were under way, Zoe scanned the other passengers. She was sure there had to be at least one police officer on board with them besides Mort, but she couldn't pick anyone out who looked like law enforcement.

They cleared the harbor, and the wind whipped her hair around, blinding her. She scraped it off her face, twisted it over her shoulder, and held it there with one hand. Jack stretched his arm along the back of the bench and said in a voice that she could barely hear above the wind and engine noise, "You know they'll want to use you as bait."

"I'm not the bait, the painting is."

Jack looked at her steadily. "You don't have to do it. They

can get a female police stand-in. Someone who looks like you."

"Yeah, red hair is so common here."

"They do have wigs in Italy."

"What if Gray sends Oscar? He knows me. An imposter won't fool him."

"It's not a good idea," Jack insisted.

She twisted toward him. "Jack, I have to do it. There is no way I'm letting anyone else hold that painting. I don't care how trustworthy they tell me someone is. A painting worth twelve million dollars might be too much temptation to resist."

Jack opened his mouth to argue, but Zoe cut him off. "I'm doing it." Jack was already squinting in the bright sun, but his eyes slitted even more.

She put her hand on his arm. "Think what it will mean. This mess will be over. You've been cleared of fraud charges, the money's been traced to the painting, and now they know I didn't take the money. If Gray is arrested, we're in the clear. There's nothing else to come back and bite us. It's over. We can go on. We can look forward instead of always looking back over our shoulders."

"Right. That's the main thing. To go forward and forget all this mess," he said, his voice tight.

"Jack, I didn't mean it that way."

"We're here."

Zoe had been so involved in the conversation she hadn't realized they were alongside the cruise ship. She huffed a sigh of frustration and followed Jack's stiff back up the stairs. They swiped in and silently went to the customer service area where the security deposit boxes were located. Mort had boarded ahead of them, and they trailed him down the passageways. Once they were in the vault area, Mort nodded to them both, then introduced a man with close cropped dark brown hair who wore a tight polo shirt straining across a muscular chest and arms, plaid shorts, and espadrilles. "This is Major Cornelio Avera of the Italian Art Squad. He's here to assess the painting and escort us back to Capri."

Zoe recognized him. He'd been on the tender with them, but she would have never thought he was a cop. He removed his aviator sunglasses and nodded briefly, but his attention was on the safety deposit box that had just been placed on a table in the middle of the room. The cruise ship attendant left, closing the door behind her.

The room was small to begin with, and with four people, one of them as burly as Avera, the fit was extremely tight. Zoe bumped her elbows with Jack and Avera as she pulled the key off the chain around her neck. Avera perched his sunglasses on his head and pulled on a pair of white gloves. He waited, his hands held up like a surgeon ready for the operating room.

Zoe opened the box and removed the plastic bag, then took out the first painting, the Monet. This was it, she thought, twisting the necklace chain through her fingers. If she'd taken the wrong painting... If it wasn't really a Monet...

Zoe wasn't sure, but she thought she saw a tiny, involuntary smile as Avera bent over the painting with a small magnifying glass. "*Bella*," he murmured. Zoe relaxed and dropped the chain. She saw she'd been squeezing it so tightly that the ring had left an imprint in her palm.

Avera carefully detached the clips and turned the painting over to examine the back, and then he stood. "It is a beautiful painting and appears to be the missing Monet."

"Appears?" Zoe asked.

"I cannot verify it here, under these circumstances. That will require testing and more comparison, but I am satisfied."

Mort said, "If Avera is satisfied, you have nothing to worry about."

"What is this?" Avera removed the second painting from the plastic bag.

"A fake. One from the villa we told you about," Zoe said.

"Ah, yes," Avera said, "The villa of bad art, we are calling it."

"You've seen it?" Jack asked.

"Oh, yes. I came from there. The fire brigade contacted us. They had to enter the villa to ensure that all the people were out. They saw the room of identical paintings." He shrugged. "Suspicious, no?"

"Yes, very," Zoe agreed. "Were Anna and the man...what was his name?" She looked to Jack.

"Giorgio. Were they still there?"

"Yes. The fire brigade kept them from reentering the property until we arrived. Once we secured the area, we took them into custody."

Mort said, "Avera confirmed what you told the police about the villa. That went a long way toward establishing your credibility last night."

"Do you know about Anna's travel? Her trip to Paris and the one to Dubai? We wondered if she'd tried to sell a copy of the painting in Dubai."

"Her sales trips, yes. We are gathering details. She delivered a painting to a gallery in Dubai and then shortly after bought the villa. It appears the switch went so well they decided to try it again, thinking that going to a different geographic region would protect them from detection."

"Have you contacted the dealer she approached in Paris, Masard?"

"Interpol has spoken with him," Avera said. "He's identified a photo of Anna Whitmore as the woman who attempted to sell the fake, not you. Another plus in your column."

"What will happen to him?"

"Masard?" Mort asked. "Nothing, I imagine."

Avera nodded. "He's done nothing wrong. He did not pay for the painting, and he contacted authorities. I realize he helped you out, by delaying contact with the police, but he is a good source for us to have." He checked his watch. "We must get you and the painting back to Capri for the meeting."

21

Zoe stood in front of Dock Five, wishing she'd brought her hat. The hot rays of the sun beat down on her and she could almost feel her skin tightening, shrinking away from the brilliant glare. She and Jack hadn't spoken since their argument on the tender. Before she'd left for the dock, he'd wished her good luck, but his tone had been so reserved that she almost wished he hadn't said anything. His quiet formality crushed her. She wanted his light banter and reassuring smile, but she only had herself to blame. She was the one who pushed him away.

She recognized Oscar's stiff-legged penguin-like stride as he moved between the open-top cabs ferrying tourists to their hotels. She switched the plastic bag from one hand to the other. There had been a loud debate about whether she should bring the imitation painting instead of the Monet, but Avera had finally prevailed, declaring it wasn't a good enough fake to fool an expert. If Gray had someone to authenticate the painting they couldn't take the risk of tipping him off too soon. The wire had also been declared too risky and removed.

"Afternoon. Hot day, isn't it?" His face was flushed, sweat beaded his hairline, and his loose golf shirt was ringed with patches of sweat under his arms.

"You picked the time."

"May I?" he indicated the plastic bag.

"I'll hold onto it," Zoe said, but opened the bag so that he could see the painting inside.

"Excellent. This way."

She followed him to a marina at one end of the harbor where he escorted her onto a small motorboat. She took a seat, and Oscar sat down beside her. Another man, who didn't speak to them, cast off and maneuvered the boat out of the harbor into the open water. As soon as they cleared the harbor walls, the boat turned left, westward, in a sweeping curve. Zoe breathed a small sigh of relief.

They were staying near Capri, not cutting across the water to Naples. The police had several plans ready, each one set up for a different scenario, but Zoe didn't like the idea of trekking across the open bay with only Oscar and the silent captain.

She kept one hand on the painting and clasped the other over the clip in her hair at the back of her head, a perfectly natural reaction to the wind that teased long strands away from the clip and tossed them across her face as the captain increased their speed.

She knew there were boats in the water, watching her movements, relaying their course via radio to the back room of the restaurant along the harbor, where they'd gone over the plans one last time. Her cell phone was turned on and the tracking app was still on it. She knew Jack, still in the restaurant back room, was watching her movement on it, but he'd insisted it wasn't enough. Mort and Russo, the Carabinieri officer with the tinges of gray at his temples, had agreed.

Several options had been hotly debated—it seemed the Italians were passionate about everything, including tracking devices—but in the end, they had all agreed that the smallest was the best. A thin black square about the length of a paper-clip had been taped to the inside of the hairclip she'd found in her bag.

The boat hugged the island, cutting through the waves. Oscar's short hair pulsed against his scalp as he pointed out the Blue Grotto as if they were on a sightseeing tour. Normally, Zoe would have leaned over the edge of the boat to get a better view, but she was so tense right now that she barely glanced at the crush of rowboats grouped around the crevice where the white limestone met the sea. A layer of green vegetation covered the rise above the limestone escarp-ment like icing on a cake, the deep green contrasting sharply with the band of grayish-white limestone.

Their boat skimmed over the water and even though it was fairly calm, Zoe felt a surge of nausea. She'd never been seasick in her life, but she definitely felt queasy. The scenery whipped by, another village cascading down to the sea, then an imposing lighthouse perched on a headland, but Zoe barely glanced at them, concentrating instead on breathing steadily as she told herself the boat ride couldn't last much longer.

"The faraglioni," Oscar said, drawing her attention back to the view. "The sea stacks," he explained, pointing to the three massive rocks. One was still attached to the island, but the other two rose from the sea, weathered and rugged. The center of the middle stack had worn away, leaving an archlike opening that dwarfed the boats angling through it. The sea suddenly felt crowded and the captain cut back on their speed. Tourist boats, small motorboats, sailboats, and yachts congregated around the sea stacks. Zoe thought they were heading to the needle-like opening, but then the boat angled and made for one of the yachts, a blue and white monstrosity with three decks, jet skis, and a helicopter.

Their captain edged up to the yacht, and Oscar waved her ahead of him up a short set of stairs attached to the side of the yacht. She climbed up with one hand, keeping the painting gripped to her side. A sturdy man with a ruddy face and long greasy hair blocked her at the top. He reached for the plastic bag. Zoe shrunk away from him. There was nowhere else to go but back down the stairs, and Oscar was there below her, blocking her retreat.

"Antonio will be careful with the painting," Oscar said.

"I'm not letting go of it until I personally give it to Mr. Gray."

Antonio stepped aside, and Zoe took a step forward, surprised her little speech worked.

As she passed him, he grabbed her free arm and twisted it against her back at an angle that sent a spear of pain through her shoulder. She gasped and tried to rotate out of his grip, but he was too strong.

Oscar plucked the painting from her as she struggled. "I will keep this. I suggest you let Antonio finish his search."

What else could she do? She wasn't a match for the thuggish Antonio. She nodded, and Antonio slowly released his grip on her arm, making Zoe think of a cat lifting its paw from a mouse so it could torment the mouse. Antonio patted her clothing and even checked her shoes, but didn't even look at the clip in her hair. He motioned for her to open her messenger bag. She pulled the flap back, and he pawed around inside, then pulled out her phone. After a glance at it, he casually flicked it over the side of the boat.

"Hey! That was my phone."

Antonio grinned.

"No electronics on the boat," Oscar said as he held his arms out to be patted down.

Thank goodness she'd left her laptop on the island. Antonio didn't seem to enjoy checking Oscar for weapons or electronics, avoiding the sweaty patches on his shirt. Finally, he stepped back, and Oscar said, "This way."

He guided them to the back of the boat to a deck with a view of the sea stacks. As they walked, Zoe realized that she wasn't feeling seasick and decided it must be because the enormous boat felt so solid and still in the water. They reached the deck at the rear of the boat, where a white leather sofa larger than a king size bed and an array of chaise lounges in teak with thick white cushions were angled toward the sea stacks.

"Well done, Ms. Hunter. Well done."

Zoe turned toward the voice. She'd completely missed him. Gray had been seated under a canvas awning that stretched over an oblong table large enough to seat eight people. She recognized him from the photo she and Jack had found on-line. His bald head shone with a gleam of perspiration. He wasn't wearing a three-piece suit, but his casually expensive collared polo, khakis and leather loafers were probably almost as expensive as an off-the-rack suit.

He'd risen, leaving a china plate smeared with tomatoes and cheese alongside discarded heavy silverware and a half-full glass of wine. Oscar had stripped the plastic bag off the painting and set it on an easel positioned below the awning in a corner near an entrance to what Zoe assumed was a cabin. Oscar dropped into a seat at the table and reached for the wine and a fresh glass from one of the unused place settings.

"Have a seat, Ms. Hunter," Gray said, motioning to the table. "Wine?"

"No, thank you."

"You're sure?" he asked in an absent-minded way, his attention focused on the painting. He adjusted his circular glasses and stroked his neatly trimmed gray beard. This was an international criminal? He looked like a college professor scanning an essay. "Claudia, it's here," he called, and a woman in a white linen pantsuit with light brown hair emerged from the doorway. Zoe wasn't sure what her role was, but then she snapped on thick lensed, rectangular glasses with dark frames and pulled on white gloves as she leaned over the painting beside Gray. Ah, art expert, Zoe thought, scanning the deck and then gazing out at the water as nonchalantly as she could.

Where were they? They'd told her they would move in as soon as Gray had the painting.

Gray and the woman, Claudia, murmured in low voices. She lifted the painting and checked the back while Zoe watched Antonio circle along the edge of the deck. He moved his arm, and the hem of his shirt rose, revealing the butt of a gun tucked at his hip.

Beyond his shoulder, she saw a mid-sized gray boat heading their direction. Antonio's progress along the railing checked. It had caught his attention, too. Zoe said, "On second thought." She reached for the wine and managed to knock over both a wine glass and the bottle of wine. The glass exploded against the deck. Antonio jerked toward the sound.

The wine bottle trundled over the table, spewing ruby liquid across the china and linen. Several drops spattered onto Oscar. "Oh! Oh, my. I am so sorry," Zoe said, and she didn't have to fake her horror. How much had that wine glass cost, not to mention the wine? She lunged for the wine bottle, bumped the table, and the rest of the glasses rocked.

"Please, Ms. Hunter, have a seat." Gray left the painting and came to pull out a chair for her. He shushed Oscar, who was sputtering and daubing at his shirt.

"I am so sorry."

"Do not worry," Gray soothed. "You have brought me my Monet. What is a little wine, a broken glass? Nothing."

Already, there was a woman bending over the glass slivers, sweeping them into a dustpan.

Zoe dropped into the seat he held for her, watching the gray boat as it neared. Antonio saw it, too, and called, "Guardia di Finanza."

Gray sighed and rolled his eyes. "Yes, yes. It is too late to outrun them now. Show them the paperwork then get rid of them." He waved Antonio away then turned to Zoe. "The tax police. Such a tedious business." He picked a fresh glass and opened a new bottle of wine. "They are making a nuisance of themselves, boarding luxury yachts and checking forms. They will run off all the yachts from Italy, if they are not careful," he said with a wry smile and returned to the painting.

Zoe scanned the deck, considering her options. Mort had said the Italian authorities anticipated Gray would go quietly and set his lawyers to work, looking for loopholes. It was the way he usually operated. But Antonio had a gun, and he seemed like the type to put up a fight.

Zoe heard a muffled thump. Oscar, still occupied with his shirt, didn't look up. Neither did Gray or Claudia. Zoe set her glass down carefully and calculated the distance from her chair to the sofa. She wanted to be as far away from Gray as possible when he figured out what was going on.

It was almost anticlimactic when it happened. Four men in gray uniforms with gold-capped sleeves, two on the port side and two on the starboard side, filed onto the deck. They carried revolvers aimed at Oscar and Gray.

"Do not move," barked one of the men. Zoe saw the gray at his temples. It was Russo, but she didn't have time to look at anyone else before Gray's laughter drew her attention back to him.

"The tax police? This is truly entertaining—it will make a fabulous dinner party story—but I assure you, my paperwork is in order. You have no issue with me. I am a law-abiding citizen."

"I think not, *Signore* Gray." Russo placed one hand on his chest. "You see, we are the Carabinieri, and they," he pointed to his companions, "are with Interpol."

A flicker passed over Gray's face and while all attention was on him, Oscar jumped up from the table. Zoe stood, too, backing away from the table and out of Oscar's range, but he barreled into the Carabinieri officer, who squared up to meet the blow. It looked like Oscar ricocheted off a wall. He rebounded, arms flailing, but another gray uniformed man restrained Oscar even before he regained his balance.

While that commotion was going on, Gray spun, grabbed the Monet, and flung it as hard as he could toward Zoe, aiming high so that it would sail over her head, past the railing, and into the sea. The square of cardboard it was attached to spun through the air, pin wheeling over Zoe's head, the canvas flickering in the wind.

Zoe took two steps back, extended her arms and jumped. Her hands came together over her head, closing in a slap that fastened the cardboard and canvas between her palms, but an instant later her hip hit the railing, and she began to tip. A hand gripped her shoulder and yanked her back to the deck.

It was Sato's face above the gray uniform. "Good catch."

"BUT why did he try to throw it overboard?" Kathy asked.

She and Mort had asked Sato, Zoe, and Jack to join them for dinner. They were gathered around a restaurant table at the very edge of a terrace wedged into the slope of the hillside above the harbor and had the most spectacular view of lights of Capri harbor twinkling on the black water and the slice of moon overhead. Mort said, "It was a good diversion, but most likely, it was his attempt to get rid of the evidence."

"But he was surrounded, wasn't he?" Kathy asked, looking to Zoe.

"Yes, I'd never seen so much gray since middle school. Uncanny how the color of the uniform of the tax police is the same as the lockers that lined the hallways."

"Where's the painting now?" Kathy asked.

"The Art Squad took it out of my hands pretty fast," Zoe said.

Sato waved his fork, "They have already contacted the museum it was stolen from. Press conference tomorrow."

"And what will happen to Gray?" Kathy asked.

"I have no idea," Zoe said with a shrug. "All I know is that I spent the last four hours answering questions about what happened on Gray's boat, and Jack and I are now free to leave Capri and Italy." She glanced at Jack, who was seated across the table from her, and he raised his glass of wine to her in a toast and smiled, but the gesture seemed perfunctory, his smile automatic. Zoe looked quickly away, her heart shriveling. She should have been ecstatic. It was over. She and Jack were in the clear, but she felt flat and empty.

This afternoon when she returned to the harbor with the entourage that included a restrained Gray, along with Oscar, Antonio, and Claudia, she'd seen worry on his face as his gaze skimmed over the people entering the police station. When he'd finally seen her, the tension had eased from his face, but he hadn't moved across the room to embrace her. Instead, he'd stayed where he was.

Zoe had wanted to run across the room to him, but she couldn't seem to make her feet move, and then she'd been shuffled into a room and had to recount the events of the afternoon. When she'd emerged from the interviews, Kathy had swept her into the group on the way to dinner. Zoe tried to ignore the twist in her heart as Jack sipped his wine then checked his watch. "Mort and Sato know more about that," she said.

Zoe pushed the last bites of her ravioli around her plate as Mort said, "Interpol has custody. They're sorting out who gets him first."

"All this fuss over him. I've never heard of him," Kathy said. "Is he really such an important guy?"

"Oh, yes," Mort said. "He's wanted in at least seven countries. He coordinates a huge crime network that involves drugs, scams, and money laundering in Europe, the United States, and Central America. He also aids and abets other criminals, helping them hide from authorities. That's what he did for Costa."

Kathy said, "And Costa intended to use the Monet as currency to pay off Gray?" she said in horrified tones. "That is so wrong. Art like that should be in a museum where it can be seen and appreciated, not shuttled around furtively. Who knows what kind of damage could have been done to it."

Mort agreed then said, "That was his plan until Anna stole it from him."

"Serves him right," Kathy muttered.

Mort looked at Zoe. "Anna knew that Costa had set you up to take the blame for purchasing and selling the stolen painting. She posed as you in Paris to protect herself. She had no idea that Gray had quietly put out the word that he wanted to buy the painting if it became available. He never intended to buy it. He only wanted the information on who had it, so he could get back what he saw as his property."

"What an awful person," Kathy said.

Sato, who had been concentrating on his steak, put his silverware down with a satisfied sigh, then added, "As bad as the art crime was, don't forget he's accused of money laundering, tax evasion, murder, and—" he broke off and pulled his phone from his pocket. "Excuse me," he said, leaning back in his chair to read a text message.

Kathy turned to Mort. "Well then, I guess I'll have to forgive you for missing the last few days of our vacation."

"There's still tonight and tomorrow," Mort said. "Plenty of time to play bridge."

"Forget bridge. I know you hate it. But I will hold you to at least one more dance," Kathy said then caught sight of Sato's phone. "Is that a baby," she asked in the tone one would use to ask if pigs were flying.

"Yes. My new partner's first, a girl." Sato handed her the phone and she oohed and awed.

"Alexandra Lynn. Guess I'll have to stop calling him a kid," Sato said in a regretful tone.

Mort said, "Now you can call him Pops."

Sato looked more cheerful. "That's true."

"Oh, a text just came in," Kathy said, handing the phone back. "Jenny."

Mort raised his eyebrows. "Jenny Singletarry?"

"Yeah. She probably wants an interview." Zoe thought she saw a fleeting smile on Sato's face. No, that couldn't be right. There was no way he would look forward to talking to a reporter. And Jenny was not his style at all, but Mort was studying Sato with a thoughtful look, too. She filed it away. Zoe knew Jenny would have tons of questions for her when news of Gray's arrest broke. Zoe figured she could work in a question of her own.

An hour later, Sato insisted on paying the bill, and the dinner party broke up with Sato returning to wrap up final details with the Italian police and Interpol. Mort, Kathy, Jack, and Zoe clambered aboard the last tender to take them back to the cruise ship, which was scheduled to depart during the night for Rome, the final destination of the cruise.

"Do you think we'll be able to get back on the ship?" Zoe asked.

Jack shrugged. "I wouldn't be surprised if the crew is more vigilant than last night."

"I hope they'll at least let us pick up our belongings we left in the cabin." And they needed to arrange for Paul and Isobel's belongings to be taken ashore in Rome and transferred to the airport.

"I think you'll have a very different reception," Mort said

as he and Jack waved Zoe and Kathy into the last two seats, while the men stood. Zoe wanted to talk to Jack, but wedged into the crowded boat was clearly not the place to do it.

Once they reached the cruise ship, the captain waited at the top of the stairs, but he was beaming, not glowering at them.

Mort said, "He's been briefed about what happened, and he's happy to take credit for the involvement of his ship in bringing an international criminal to justice."

Arms thrown wide, the captain welcomed them to the ship in both Italian and English, then informed Zoe and Jack that they were special guests, and he hoped they would honor them with their presence on the short trip to Rome. Their "borrowed" cabin and the entire ship were at their disposal. Jack was silent, so Zoe accepted on their behalf and thanked the captain. He bowed over her hand. "No, the honor is ours."

"I expect cameras and a press conference tomorrow," Mort said under his breath as they moved away. They passed through the multi-story open atrium, then Zoe stopped at the turn in the passageway that led to the staircase to their cabin. "Well, in case I don't see you tomorrow, thank you for everything," she said to Mort. "I literally could not have done it without you."

Mort waved her words away. "I just made a few phone calls."

"It was more than that."

"Not really. Besides, it livened things up just when the cruise was getting a tad boring." He rubbed his hands together and looked at Kathy. "Now, I believe I owe you a dance?"

"Indeed you do. To the dance floor." Kathy tucked her

arm through his elbow and gave Zoe a wave as they headed away. Zoe smiled after them, then turned and looked for Jack, but he was gone. She twisted around, scanning the passageway, but he'd disappeared. Frowning, she made her way to the cabin, only taking two wrong turns.

She pushed open the door. "Jack?" The room was empty. Her messenger bag rested on the end of the bed beside a folded piece of paper with her name. She snatched it up.

Zoe,

I have collected my clothes and arranged for the cabin steward to pack Paul and Isobel's things and transfer them to the Rome airport tomorrow.

I am bowing out of your life now. I had hoped you'd change your mind, but I can see that isn't going to happen, so instead of making more of a fool of myself, I'm leaving tonight. I'll change the return on my airline ticket. I'll have my stuff out of the house by the time you get back. I will miss you, but wish you every happiness.

Jack

Zoe blinked at the paper for a second, then dropped it, yanked open the door, and sprinted along the passageway to the stairs. She took them two at a time, racing toward the main atrium area of the ship. Jack would have to go through there to get back to the tender. Was the tender even running to shore again? Maybe he wouldn't be able to get off the ship. Or, had he arranged for another boat to pick him up?

She pushed hard up the last few steps and dashed into the atrium, only to stop, panting as she scanned the people strolling through the multi-floor open area of shops and restaurants. How could she spot him? It was a massive space with balconies rising layer on layer up to the glass ceiling overhead.

Then she saw him. His back was to her, and he was rising smoothly up one of the escalators to the next deck, the plastic bag of his clothes in one hand.

"Jack!" she shouted and made for the escalator. He didn't hear her. Her words floated into the open air and were drowned in the vortex of chatter and piped-in music. She cut off a couple about to step on the escalator and did the double stair climb again, pushing around people. He was almost to the top, and she was only half way up. "Jack, wait!"

He turned as he stepped off, spotted her, and moved to the railing that enclosed the balcony as he called, "Zoe, we've already said everything there is to say,"

"No, we haven't. Or, I haven't." She sprinted up the last stairs and burst off the top step to join Jack at the railing. "I've finally figured out I love you."

Zoe was vaguely aware that as the people came off the escalator, some were lingering, watching them, along with some other curious onlookers, but she didn't care about them. Jack's guarded expression didn't change.

Zoe gripped the railing. "Too sudden?" He didn't say anything, so she rushed on, ignoring the cold knot of dread inside. "This wasn't really how I'd planned to tell you. Actually, I didn't have a plan. I didn't know how to tell you."

"That you love me?"

"Yes," she said firmly.

One corner of his mouth crept up. "What brought this on?"

"I had a lot of time to think on that beach. I don't want to shy away from...this...from you. When I said I wanted us to be able to move on from everything that had happened, I didn't mean move on with each of us going our separate ways. I meant together. Now we can put all the baggage—the lies and secrets—behind us." She swallowed. "I hope it's not too late. I hope you'll give us another chance. You know me, the real me, and you still like me. Which is unbelievable, when I think about it. I know you now, Jack. I like you."

"I thought you loved me," Jack said.

"I do. I love you, *and* I like you. Well, don't just stand there."

His half-smile widened and his expression softened. "All right." He dropped the bag and closed the distance between them, his hands sliding into her hair at the back of her neck, holding her close as he kissed her. Zoe wrapped her arms around his shoulders and felt the tight core of fear that had been inside her burst into a million pieces and evaporate. When the kiss ended, Zoe slowly opened her eyes and said, "Well?"

"What?"

"Do you love me?"

He leaned back. "It wasn't obvious from the kiss? Hmm... better do it again."

"No. Words."

"I love you, Zoe Hunter." She smiled and leaned forward to kiss him again when she came back down to earth long enough to hear a chorus of *aww*. She froze. "People are staring."

"Let them. I don't care.

"I think that woman is recording us on her phone."

"Perhaps a change of scene is in order." Jack picked up the bag, and they linked hands, moving to the doors that opened onto the exterior deck. A cool breeze swept over them as they walked to a deserted area at the railing. A thin strip of moonlight danced along the waves, and the lights of Capri sparkled in the distance.

Jack gathered her back into his arms and leaned against the railing for a lingering kiss. Eventually, he said, "Let's get a few things sorted right off the bat," as he dropped a trail of kisses along Zoe's neck. "We're not going to mess this up. First, no secrets and no divorce."

"I like it."

"Good." The wind whipped a strand of hair across Zoe's face, and Jack tucked it behind her ear. "Now, when are you going to marry me?" He kissed her cheek, then the corner of her mouth. "Next month? Next year?"

"Why wait? Let's do it tonight," Zoe said, lightly. "We're on a ship. We have a captain to marry us, and he did say the ship was at our disposal. We even have a ring. It can be our something old. Mort and Kathy can be our witnesses."

"That is so like you, to dive right in."

"Why not?" She turned serious. "I'm all in. We can get married tonight or six months from now, doesn't make any difference to me. I'm not changing my mind."

"Well, let's get married tonight, by all means."

He leaned down to kiss her, then pulled back slightly. "This is quite a one-eighty for you, you know. Are you sure?"

"Yes." She smiled at him. "I think I've loved you for a long time. I started figuring it out when I was alone on that beach. Tonight confirmed it for me. I should have been thrilled—we're in the clear, and no one is going to interfere in our lives again, but I couldn't enjoy it because we weren't together. I wanted to share that feeling with you. It wasn't the same alone. I'm not saying I'm not a little afraid. I'm terrified, actually. No, that's not quite right. It's like a rollercoaster ride, exhilarating and terrifying at the same time, but you know what? I like rollercoasters." She kissed him quickly. "I *like* risks."

"Excellent. I'm discovering I have a fondness for them, too." After a while he said, "You know, I hear Rome is an excellent place for a honeymoon."

"Hmm...the Eternal City. Sounds perfect."

THE ADVENTURE CONTINUES...

Get the Next Book: Suspicious (On the Run Book Four)

Zoe and Jack's trip to Rome was supposed to be a romantic one-year anniversary celebration with a little business on the side. Jack's fledgling security company has landed the plum assignment of providing additional security for the opening night gala of a museum exhibit featuring priceless gems.

However, the easy job turns complicated when they discover the exhibit is the next target of a cat burglar who has struck several times in recent months, snatching up a hoard of sparkling jewels. Opening night goes off without a hitch, but then the police accuse them of switching the real gems for fakes.

With the exhibit's organizer missing and planted diamonds showing up in their belongings, Zoe and Jack are forced to delve into the shady side of the diamond trade in a search for the culprit, a journey that takes them from the fountains and piazzas of the Eternal City to the snow-capped Alps.

THE STORY BEHIND THE STORY

This is my third outing with Zoe and Jack, and I've enjoyed writing it just as much as the other books. I hope you enjoyed it, too.

A few interesting notes on the story: The Impressionist painting in *Deceptive* isn't a figment of my imagination. Claude Monet's *Marine* was stolen in a 2006 heist from a museum in Rio. I hope someday I'll be able to change this note and tell you it has been found. The duty and custom free locations called free ports described in the story are real as well and must be some of the most valuable real estate on the planet. My research into tracking apps was interesting, if a little scary. Never lend your phone to someone you don't trust implicitly! Some readers may wonder about the mention of gypsies in Naples. Italy has a large gypsy population. They ask for handouts at airports, train stations, and tollbooths. Others wash windows at intersections for spare change or become street vendors, selling trinkets on beaches and street corners, doing their best to avoid the tax police.

One of the things I enjoy most about the *On The Run*

series is writing about amazing places. I was lucky enough to visit Paris for a short time and also spent several months in Italy recently. This blog has the background on my Paris research trip. I think the Amalfi Coast and Capri are two of the most gorgeous places on earth—and the first time I saw Amalfi was a gloomy, rainy day, so that tells you how beautiful it is. While Anna's villa is made-up, Jeranto beach isn't. One long sweaty afternoon, I hiked the trail to the secluded, stunning beach. So worth the work to get there!

To see more on the places that inspired me and some of my research links, check out my *Deceptive pinboard* at Pinterest. You can find out more about me and my books at my website, or you can sign up for my updates at SaraRosett.com/signup. You can find me on Twitter, Facebook or Instagram, too. Happy reading!

ACKNOWLEDGMENTS

A big thank you to everyone who read the first two books and came back to find out what happened with Zoe and Jack. Thank you so much! If you enjoyed *Deceptive*, I hope you'll help me spread the word about the series by telling your friends or reviewing the book. Those things really make a difference!

OTHER BOOKS BY SARA ROSETT

This is Sara's complete catalogue at the time of publication, but new books are in the works. To be the first to find out when Sara has a new book, sign up for her updates.

***On the Run* series**

Elusive

Secretive

Deceptive

Suspicious

Devious

Treacherous

***Murder on Location* series**

Death in the English Countryside

Death in an English Cottage

Death in a Stately Home

Death in an Elegant City

Menace at the Christmas Market (novella)

Death in an English Garden

Death at an English Wedding

High Society Lady Detective series

Murder at Archly Manor

Murder at Blackburn Hall

The Egyptian Antiquities Murder

***Ellie Avery* series**

Moving is Murder

Staying Home is a Killer

Getting Away is Deadly

Magnolias, Moonlight, and Murder

Mint Juleps, Mayhem, and Murder

Mimosas, Mischief, and Murder

Mistletoe, Merriment, and Murder

Milkshakes, Mermaids, and Murder

Marriage, Monsters-in-law, and Murder

Mother's Day, Muffins, and Murder